JOURNEY TO ZENTOBIA

STACY D'ALESSANDRO

ISBN: 978-0-578-78171-6

Cover design by: Kim Dingwall

Printed in the United States of America

This book is dedicated to my daughter

Spying without getting caught took practice. Maggie and her older brother, Peter, had a foolproof routine of snooping on their mysterious neighbor, until the morning things went drastically wrong.

The day started like every other gloomy day in Hailsville, the peculiar town their family had moved to after Maggie's dad took a job at the police station. She'd described it as Groundhog's Day in her journal, which she wrote in daily to document her new life.

Pretending to be a detective like her dad had proved her only source of fun since arriving in Hailsville three months ago. She'd convinced her brother to go along with the game, even though he would rather play basketball, or anything else, instead of amateur spying. Their first big assignment since the charade began: find out more about the man next door, Mr. Drop.

They left their house that morning after Maggie spotted him heading out for his walk.

"He looks like he's on a mission every time he leaves. I

think he's looking for something." Maggie tucked her journal close to her chest, grabbed her backpack, and walked down the front porch steps. "He's always searching in the sky, which makes no sense, since it's just filled with clouds."

"What could he be looking for?" Peter asked. "It's not like he could lose something up there. Maybe today we'll get some answers. Let's go, and don't get too close."

"I know the drill."

Their perky dog, Bacon, tagged along. The fluffy tan-and-white pup needed practice walking on a leash, so Peter often trained him while they walked. Unfortunately, Maggie liked to take Bacon off the leash to play, so their walk usually ended with a chase to bring him back.

"Look. He's turning up Olive Street. Must be taking a different route today." Peter pulled Maggie behind a thick tree to hide. She picked up Bacon and took off his leash. Normally, Mr. Drop walked down Spencer Road past the elementary school and through nearby neighborhoods, where they could dash into open garages to hide. Their sleuth-like antics often found them ducking behind smelly garbage cans and even climbing up porch steps, where they hid behind unlocked gates. "He's headed closer to town. There won't be anything to cover us if he goes much farther."

"Strange. He's never gone this way before." She put Bacon down and wrote a description of the new route. "Maybe he's meeting someone. Keep an eye out for other people."

Mr. Drop picked up his pace on the cracked sidewalk as the town's only cluster of historic, tall buildings appeared in the distance.

"He's moving faster than usual. Probably because it's about to rain again." Peter grabbed her arm and tugged her along. "Finish that later. Where's Bacon?"

A bark from somewhere ahead caught Maggie's attention. A woman with a giant dog on a leash headed their direction. Bacon darted straight for the dog.

"Oh no! Bacon will pass Mr. Drop to get to that dog." Maggie bolted to catch up to the pooch. "Hurry, before he recognizes Bacon and sees us!"

Peter's middle-school track skills helped, but not enough to reach Bacon before he bumped into Mr. Drop, causing him to trip. He caught himself from falling flat on his face. The pup kept running until he exchanged loud barks with the massive dog ahead.

Maggie threw her journal inside her backpack, took the leash out, and attached it to Bacon's collar. "I'm sorry. Our dog loves to meet new friends. Come on, Bacon. Let's go."

The woman tried to control her furry beast as it slobbered all over Bacon's face.

Maggie turned around to see Mr. Drop heading straight toward them, his extra-long mustache overwhelming his face as he walked. She lowered her eyes. *Oh, no. We're caught.*

"Maggie, Peter...It's nice to see you and your overexcited dog." Bacon jumped at Mr. Drop's sensible walking trousers. Before Bacon could tear a hole in them, he pulled a dog treat out of his pocket and placed it a few inches away on the ground. "What are you doing here?"

Never at a loss for words, Maggie said, "We're on an assignment for school that we had to get done early this morning. What are you doing?" *Why not just ask where he goes? Maybe he'll give us a clue.*

Thunder boomed in the distance. A bolt of lightning

flashed, illuminating the gold-rimmed circular glasses on Mr. Drop's plump face.

"I like to explore and look for things I've never seen before, and discover things I thought were lost."

What a weird answer. What did he lose?

Peter pointed to the thick, gray clouds. "Oh, boy, this looks like it's going to be a big storm." Small water droplets landed on his forehead, and he wiped them off with the back of his hand. "It was nice running into you, but we better go before it pours. We forgot an umbrella."

Peter picked up Bacon, and they waved goodbye before Mr. Drop asked them any more questions.

Maggie's heart pounded as she ran down the street. She stopped to catch her breath. "That was close. Good idea to say we forgot our umbrella."

"That was a disaster." Their house came into view up ahead. "Bacon almost ran the guy over. You shouldn't have taken him off the leash. I think we should stop following him for a while."

"No way. There's nothing else to do, and I want to solve this case. Besides, we found out more information today than we have since we started following him a month ago. We now know he is an explorer looking for something like an ancient artifact."

"You figured that out from his weird comment about discovering things that he thought were lost?"

"Yep." She ran up the front porch and opened the door to the smell of her mom's home cooking.

"That makes no sense. He might be some kind of explorer, but probably more like a bird watcher or someone that studies clouds. I doubt there are any ancient artifacts in Hailsville," Peter said.

Maggie walked into the kitchen. Peter trailed behind.

"Where have you been? It looks like a storm is coming," their mom said. Storms in Hailsville brewed more frequently than their mom's coffee. "Come inside and have a quick breakfast. We have a little time before school. I'm substituting for Mr. Taylor's class today."

Maggie liked when her mom substituted at her school, because then she didn't have to take the bus. The bus ride could be hard for a new kid, especially a ten-year-old who didn't have any friends yet. She usually sat by herself and kept a low profile, trying to figure out who the popular kids were and which mean ones to avoid.

She took a seat at the table to eat. "Um...Mom, do you know why Mr. Drop goes walking every morning?"

Her mom looked at Maggie across the counter. "I have no idea. Why? He was very nice when we moved in. But we've only talked a couple of times since then. I think your father has spent more time with him."

"Let's invite the guy over for dinner," Peter blurted as he went to the sink to wash his hands. "Then Maggie can ask him all the questions she wants."

"Hey! Are you calling me nosy? You would never ask him to come over. You're too shy."

"I might be a little shy, but yeah, you're nosy." He dried his hands on his favorite dark blue jeans, which were becoming too short for his growing thirteen-year-old frame. "Maybe we can at least find out why it rains all the time in this town. I bet they named Hailsville after all the rain. Does the sun even exist here? Because I can't remember what it looks like."

"I sort of do. Right after we moved here, we hiked with Bacon. It was super sunny outside, and there was a rainbow.

I remember because we kept saying how excited we were to see the sun."

Peter's face lit up. "Oh, yeah, and you thought we were being followed and kept looking behind you."

"We were being followed. I know it."

"Whatever. All I know is I got a leg cramp from you taking forever to write stuff in your journal. Even Bacon got bored and made friends with the stray cats."

Maggie brought her leather-bound journal everywhere. It not only had a fancy letter M with sparkles and shine in the middle of the cover, but her grandmother had given it to her as a gift before she passed away. Maggie used it to document things and jot down ideas. Especially all the information and clues she gathered to help solve the cases she worked on with her brother.

Their mom's loud sigh interrupted them. "Stop fighting. I know it's gloomy here, and it's not the best situation right now." She cleared the table. "But remember, this is a great opportunity for your father. He's taking on a big role as a detective at the police department here. I think this town could grow on all of us. We just need to give it a little time."

"I sure hope so, because there's nothing to do here," Peter said.

Maggie felt sorry for her brother. He lacked self-confidence, and being in a new town with unfamiliar people didn't help him step out of his shell.

Their dad walked into the kitchen. His worn shoes squeaked on the linoleum.

"Dad! We were just talking about you," Peter said.

"Yeah, we don't like it here," Maggie said.

"Well, good morning to you guys too." Dad put his briefcase down and hugged the kids. "It's hard moving and meeting new people. It's a change for all of us. But I have a feeling things will get better, and you guys will have fun."

Maggie wasn't sure this would be the case, but since her stomach rumbled from the walk, she didn't want to debate. "I hope so. Can we eat?"

A roar of thunder echoed through the house, and the lights flickered.

"I'll get the candles ready in case the electricity goes out," their mom said.

Before she could retrieve them, the home phone rang. She pushed her long brown hair behind her ears and answered the call. After exchanging a quick hello, she glanced over at Peter. "It's for you."

"For me?" He walked over to the phone. "Who calls me? I don't know anyone." He took the phone. "Hello? Uh-huh. Okay. Um, sure. I'll ask Maggie and my parents, and we'll try to come by after dinner. Okay, bye."

He hung up, his mouth wide open. He turned to his family. "You will not believe this, but that was Mr. Drop. He wants Maggie and me to come over for some dessert tonight. He said he'll have hot chocolate and cookies."

"No way," Maggie said. "I'm not going. Why is he inviting us to his house?" A lump formed in her throat, and her breath quickened. *Yikes! Did he figure out we were spying on him? Is he going to tell Mom and Dad?*

Mom spoke up. "I think he might be lonely. But we don't know him well enough to send you guys over there alone."

"Plus, there's a storm coming, the lights could go out, and he could lock us in a basement," Maggie said.

"I'm sure that wouldn't happen. Well, maybe the lights will go out. Go ahead and have breakfast, and we'll head to school. Your dad and I will walk you to his house later, and we'll all get to know him a little better."

Maggie begrudgingly agreed and put her journal in her backpack. As she zipped her bag, another clap of thunder crashed above their heads, and the lights went out.

"Great, I hope the electricity comes back on before tonight," Peter said.

CHAPTER TWO

Water droplets bounced off Maggie's umbrella on the brief walk to Mr. Drop's house that evening. As they approached, she asked her mother to hold the umbrella over her head so she could take out her journal from her backpack.

"What can you possibly be writing?" Peter said. "We haven't even gotten inside yet."

"I'm documenting the outside of his home. There are lots of little details I want to record. For example, look, he left his window open and it's raining." She peered inside. "He's asleep! We better leave." She turned around.

Her mom grabbed her arm. "He invited you over, so I'm sure he'll be okay with waking up." She knocked on the door.

"No answer. Let's go." Maggie turned to leave again.

Before she could move another muscle, the door creaked open, and Mr. Drop appeared. She stared at his thick mustache, wondering if it could reach his ears if he pushed it all the way back. She noted his full head of wavy black-and-gray hair and piercing green eyes and decided she would write all about his appearance in her journal later that evening. *Remembering details about someone's appearance is an important skill in being a detective.*

"Hello, Mr. Drop. It's so nice of you to invite the kids over to visit. We always like to get to know our neighbors better. I think they could use the company, too," Maggie's dad said.

"I'm happy to have them. I see the kids chasing after their little dog in my yard all the time and thought we could all get better acquainted. I don't get to see my grandkids anymore. They're too far away."

"Sorry to hear that." Mom poked her head inside the dark room. "Where do they live?"

He averted his eyes. "Why don't you all come inside out of the rain, and I can get the kids some hot chocolate." He ushered them in and turned on the lights.

The decor took Maggie's breath away. Green-and-yellow wallpaper and knickknacks of animals, bugs, birds, butterflies, and fish—all things you didn't see much of in Hailsville—stood on small tables and shelves.

"Wow, this place is straight out of a page of a *National Geographic* Encyclopedia," Peter said. He walked around the small room, reaching out to touch all the little animal figurines.

A large painting of a rainbow with colors so bright you needed sunglasses to look at it hung on the center of the living room wall. Maggie wondered if Mr. Drop had painted it himself and why he would have such a picture smack dab in the middle of the wall.

"Look at all these little animal statues." Maggie scribbled as fast as she could into her journal. "I hope you don't mind if I take notes. I like to document things for reference later."

"Yeah, every single thing," Peter said, stopping in front of the rainbow painting. "How about that hot chocolate?"

Mr. Drop smiled at the boy as he walked over and stood next to Maggie, who ignored her brother's sarcasm. "That's a wonderful idea to write things down." He glanced at her notebook. "How long have you been doing that?"

"Ever since we moved here a few months ago. The town we moved from was really modern. It seems like in Hailsville we've gone back in time. I bet it's been years since they built anything new."

"Yeah, don't they have workers to fix all the cracks in the sidewalks and streets?" Peter asked.

Mr. Drop shook his head. "Hailsville is a little outdated. But the people are friendly enough, and there's a great bakery on the corner of Cherry Lane and Peacock Avenue. They even deliver. I'll go get that hot chocolate."

"Great. Do you have any pastries from that bakery?" Peter asked.

"Sorry, I'm fresh out." He went to the kitchen.

"Darn," Peter said. "I think I know what bakery he's talking about, and it's really good."

"That was very bold of you to ask," Maggie said.

"Well, we didn't have dessert, and I want something sweet besides the drink."

While the kids were talking, their mom said to their dad, "Mr. Drop seems like a sweet man who misses spending time with his grandchildren. How do you feel about leaving the kids and coming back for them in a bit?"

"The time I've spent with him has been pleasant, and he seems harmless. But I would feel better if we knew a little more about him."

"That's what we'll find out when you leave," said Maggie, eavesdropping.

"You know I don't find that funny. You guys are not real detectives and can't go snooping around someone's house."

"Who said anything about snooping? I agree with Mom. He probably misses his grandkids. We'll be fine," Peter said.

Their dad's phone rang, and he answered it. He mumbled something and hung up. "Looks like you get to stay. Your mom and I have to run to Aunt Stella's house." He turned to their mom. "She has a leak in her roof, which caused some flooding."

"That's terrible," their mom said. She put a hand on Peter's shoulder. "Stay out of trouble. We'll be back for you soon."

Their parents called out a loud goodbye to Mr. Drop while he prepared the hot chocolate in the kitchen. The door creaked open, and they showed themselves out.

Maggie went from animal statue to animal statue, describing each item in her journal. She pointed to the art on the wall. "Peter, does this look familiar?"

"Um, yeah, because all rainbows look exactly alike. Same colors, same shape, blah blah."

"I mean the rock formations on the ground look like something we've seen before. But I can't remember where. I bet it's in my notebook." She rifled through the pages.

Mr. Drop entered with a tray of hot chocolate and marshmallows.

"So, what's the deal with the painting on your wall and all the animal statues?" Peter asked.

Mr. Drop remained silent. After placing the tray on a table in the middle of the room, he gestured for the kids to have a seat.

Maggie's apprehension from when she'd first entered the home disappeared. She could tell Peter wanted to conduct a more thorough investigation on Mr. Drop, too.

CHAPTER THREE

"How long have you lived here? How long did it take to collect all this stuff, and how much does all this cost?" Peter asked Mr. Drop.

"Whoa...slow down. I can't write that fast." Maggie shook her hand to ease the ache from jotting down so many questions. "I thought you said *I* was nosy."

Mr. Drop handed them cups, which released the aroma of fresh baked brownies. Maggie's mouth watered. They each took a sip and placed their drink on the table in front of them.

"Let's see here. That's a lot to answer," Mr. Drop said. "You're very curious, Peter. That's an excellent trait to have." He walked over to a small table covered with miniature animals and picked up a frog. He looked at Peter, then turned his attention back to the frog.

Peter slumped into the couch and ran a hand through his neatly trimmed, thick brown hair.

"These animals remind me of my childhood. I used to swim in a stream filled with frogs. They would jump from one leaf to another. This rabbit looks just like a little one I used to chase with my friends up and down a path in a forest."

Maggie glued her eyes to Mr. Drop's face. The pen in her hand didn't move. "Where did you grow up? It sounds like a very cool place." She snapped out of her gaze and flipped the page in her notebook.

His expression shifted from happy to somber, and his eyes clouded over. He turned to face the painting.

"I grew up in a place with a rich, magical history." He straightened the collar on his carefully pressed button-down shirt. "You couldn't walk six feet without seeing a cluster of animals or a grouping of fruitful trees. And a very important rainbow filled the sky."

"Like the one on your wall?" she asked.

"Yes, just like this one. I painted this to remind me of home."

"Where is home? If it was so great, why did you leave?"

A loud clap of thunder roared through the room, and Maggie and Peter jumped. Peter's knee hit his mug of hot chocolate, and some of it spilled on the table.

"I'm sorry," Peter said.

"It's okay. Let me get a towel to wipe that up. I'll be right back." Mr. Drop left the room.

As soon as he left, Peter snooped from one end to the other. "He seems like a pretty cool guy, but really weird too." He began at the end table next to the couch, eyeing everything in sight. "I don't know anyone that likes miniature animals this much. And why didn't he tell us where he's from?" He picked up a rabbit and looked underneath it.

"What are you doing?" Maggie whispered. "Didn't Dad tell us not to snoop?"

Peter moved swiftly, searching for anything that would

catch his eye. "Since when has that stopped us from investigating. Isn't that what we do?" He stopped at a white desk with two drawers. The top one was slightly ajar. He pulled it open the rest of the way.

"Yeah, it is. But we have to be careful. We already kinda got caught once today. If he catches you, he'll tell Mom and Dad!"

Peter ignored her. He shuffled through the papers in the drawer.

"What the heck?" He motioned for Maggie to join him. "Look at this. What are these symbols? Check out the strange handwriting. It's not English, and I have seen Spanish, and this is *not* it. It could be another language, but mixed in with these symbols it looks strange." He lifted the papers high above the desk, and they tried to decipher the cryptic writing and shapes.

The sound of footsteps approaching prompted Peter to place the papers back inside the desk. A page dropped to the floor. They ran over to the couch and jumped into their seats.

Mr. Drop entered the room and wiped up the spill of hot chocolate on the table. "There, good as new." He took a seat next to Maggie. "You seem to do a lot of journaling. Have you ever written anything about a rainbow that has the same background as my painting?"

Her wide eyes stared at him. "Yes. I was just talking to Peter about that."

Mr. Drop sat up straight, his giant smile causing the overgrown mustache on his face to hang off the side of his cheeks. "You don't say. Do you know where it is?"

"I can't remember. I feel like I've been there before, and not that long ago."

"I'm happy to hear you say that, because I need your help to find it."

"What do you mean? How can we help?"

He stood and walked over to the painting, his back to the kids. "This rainbow is special." He turned to them. "Can I tell you a secret?"

Maggie loved secrets, and she prided herself on keeping them. "Sure. I'm very good with secrets."

"What I am about to tell you cannot leave this room. Do we have an agreement?"

Maggie squeezed the pen in her hand. "Yes, but can I write it down?"

"As long as no one else reads your journal."

"No one else will read it. I promise."

Mr. Drop turned to Peter. "Do you agree that you won't tell anyone?"

"Can you tell me first and then I'll decide?" Peter asked.

"Come on, Peter. That's not how secrets work," Maggie said.

"Fine. I agree."

Mr. Drop walked over to them. "I need to find this rainbow to get back home to...Zentobia."

Maggie looked down in her notebook. "How do you spell Zentobia? Wait, what is Zentobia?"

"Do you mean get home in some kind of *game*?" Peter asked. "I've never heard of the game Zentobia."

"No, it's not a game. It's a place. Another world. It's where I'm from," Mr. Drop said.

Maggie and Peter burst out laughing.

"You are funny. I didn't realize you had this kind of sense of humor," Peter said.

"I'm not joking. A rainbow brought me to Hailsville, and

I've been stuck here ever since. I need to get home to my family. They don't know what happened to me."

Maggie's pen dropped to the floor. *What the heck is this guy talking about? Does he actually think he's from another world? I don't think we have enough experience to investigate another world. But it sure would be fun!*

CHAPTER FOUR

Mr. Drop thought about his home in Zentobia more often than Bacon dug in his yard. He had arrived in Hailsville shortly before the Millers and, at first, was unaware that he had traveled to another world. His first clue came when he noticed the rainbow that filled the Zentobian sky year-round wasn't there.

After regaining his composure, he walked through the town and stumbled upon a restaurant. He opened the door to the smell of something so sweet it made his mouth water. A hostess showed him where to sit and gave him a menu. After looking it over, he turned it upside down on the table. A man approached and sat down across from him.

"I recommend the chicken pot pie," the man said. "The mashed potatoes melt in your mouth, and the carrots are as sweet as brown sugar." The stocky man smiled at Mr. Drop. "Name's Hobbs McCall. I'm the town sheriff. Haven't seen you in Hailsville before."

Hobbs's wrinkled brown shirt hung unevenly over his snug belt, and mismatched patterned socks peered through the bottom of his stained trousers. The pointy silver star attached to his shirt displayed the word "sheriff."

"Well...um...yes, I just got to town and am finding my way around. I'm...Drop...Mr. Ed Drop." His memory was playing tricks on him, or he'd lost it, because he couldn't remember his name. Drop came to mind, and he ran with it. "It's a nice little place so far."

After Hobbs revealed the name of the town, Mr. Drop hoped he could find out more about it. The conversation between the two remained simple. Telling a strange man that he skipped work that morning to investigate a broken rainbow that had transported him through a portal to Hailsville might not make the best first impression. Hobbs didn't mention whether a rainbow connected Hailsville to another world either. Mr. Drop would have to find that out on his own.

When Mr. Drop said that he didn't have a place to live, the sheriff offered him a job taking care of his second home. He gratefully accepted the offer, looking forward to having a place to stay while he tried to find his way back to Zentobia. After the two ironed out the details, Hobbs put him in a cab that took him straight to his new home. Since then, he'd only seen the sheriff a handful of times.

A few months ago, when the Millers moved in next door, he had observed Maggie and Peter coming and going with their dog. He thought Maggie looked just like his granddaughter. Her small face peered through frayed brown curls that needed to be brushed. The plastic tortoise-rimmed glasses that she constantly pushed up on her nose complimented her hazel eyes.

One day, he followed the kids to see where they would go. When he got close enough, he witnessed Maggie stopping to write in what looked like a journal. *Why is she writing everything down?*

Even though he tried to stay back and hide behind trees, there were a few times he thought she might have spotted him when he got close enough to see her writing.

If she is going around town writing everything down, maybe she has documented the location of the rainbow's end. Since he had arrived in Hailsville, he had already walked down every path, turned every corner, and uncovered every stone with no luck finding the rainbow's end. *If I can befriend the kids and see her notebook, maybe it will bring back my memory. Or, I can convince her and her brother to help me search for it.*

The weather forecast predicted the biggest storm of the year to be upon them. With the powerful winds and rain, similar to what happened yearly in Zentobia, he thought it might be the best time to enlist the help of a search party. He devised a plan to fit the tight timeframe.

First, he would treat the kids to hot chocolate and share friendly stories. Next, he would invite them to join him on a walk the morning after the storm, and they would search for the location together. Once he found it, he could replicate the same scenario that had brought him to Hailsville.

The first part of the plan worked. Putting the rest of it into action halted when their mom and dad knocked at the door to pick them up.

"Looks like our parents are here." Maggie exchanged a glance with Peter. "I have so many questions about what you just told us."

He had to act fast. "I'm sure you do." He put a finger to his lips. "But, remember, don't tell anyone. Why don't you two answer the door while I straighten up here?" As soon as they went to answer the door, he grabbed Maggie's journal and stuck it under the tray of hot chocolate. Before they opened the door, he asked, "How would you like to walk together in the morning and look for the rainbow? It will be an adventure."

Maggie looked at Peter. Peter looked back and opened his mouth, but nothing came out.

The knock at the door grew louder, and Peter opened it.

Their parents stood under a large umbrella on the stoop.

"Hi. How was the visit?" their mom said.

Mr. Drop walked up behind the kids. "Your children are lovely. If it's okay with you, I would love to have them join me tomorrow for a walk. The weather should be clear in the morning, and they can even bring their little dog."

She hesitated before answering. "I don't know. They usually like to sleep in on the weekends."

Maggie grabbed her mom's arm. "Mom, we *really* want to go. We'll bring Bacon. He needs to practice walking on the leash."

"Um, yeah. Dad, this would be great training for him. Besides, it's not like I have basketball practice tomorrow. In case you forgot, I have nothing to do," Peter said.

Their dad nodded.

"Okay, sure," their mom said. "I guess that's fine."

Maggie exhaled and put on her backpack.

"Great. Meet me in front of my house at eight a.m., bright and early," Mr. Drop said.

"We'll be there. Thanks for the hot chocolate," Maggie said.

They stepped outside and made their way home.

Mr. Drop walked back to his living room to retrieve Maggie's journal. He flipped through the pages, mesmerized by her detailed notes. It might take all night to find out if she had written about the rainbow's end, but he didn't care, especially if the location was right under his nose.

CHAPTER FIVE

M aggie and Peter ran into their house and straight up to Peter's room, eager to discuss Mr. Drop.

"Well, that was interesting." Peter jumped onto his bed and took off his shoes. "What do you think Mr. Drop meant when he said he is from Zentobia? You know that's crazy, right? I mean, being from another world isn't possible."

"I know. What if he's trying to find his family, and he is confused about where they are? I hope we can find out more tomorrow." She reached for her backpack. "I'll add all that information about him to our notes."

"Maggie, Peter! Make sure you're getting ready for bed," Mom called from downstairs. "You have an early day tomorrow."

"Ugh, why did he have to say eight a.m.?" Peter said, groaning. "I hate getting up early on Saturdays. Maybe we can ask him about the symbols somehow to get more information."

"How do you figure we can do that without him knowing we snooped in his desk?" She shuffled around in her bag for the journal, but it wasn't there. Knots twisted in her stomach, and sweat formed on her brows. "OMG, I can't find my notebook. I think I left it at Mr. Drop's house! We have to go get it!"

"As long as you didn't write anything bad about him in there, who cares? You didn't, did you? It's not like it's a diary or anything."

She walked over and punched his arm.

"Ouch. What did I do?"

Her journal might not reveal her deepest, darkest secrets and feelings, but it held precious details about her lonely life in Hailsville. *I really don't want anyone to see that I eat lunch alone at school sometimes. So embarrassing.* Not only that, but it contained all the facts and clues about their cases. *How could I remember anything without it?* "You don't get it. Why do you have a problem with me writing in it?"

"I don't have a *problem* with it. I think it distracts you from making friends and from becoming a better detective. You write too much down instead of focusing on what's in front of you. Not to mention, it slows us down all the time."

Tears clouded her eyes. *Could he be right? I want to make friends here, and I want to be a better detective.*

Her mom entered the room. "Maggie, what's wrong?"

"I think I left my notebook at Mr. Drop's house, and I want it back now!" Her cries grew louder. "We have to get it." Her mom sat down next to her on the bed and smoothed back her hair.

"I'll call him and see if he found it. We can get it in the morning when we go over there. It's late now, and there's not much we can do about it tonight. You guys get ready for bed."

"Please call him now!" She stormed off to her room. The

old wooden floorboards creaking under her feet added to her frustration.

"This storm will be a big one," Maggie's dad, Griffen, said. He rummaged through kitchen drawers looking for more candles. "They say it could be the biggest of the year. Just want to make sure we're prepared."

"Good idea." Maggie's mom, Penny, called Mr. Drop, but he didn't answer.

Next door, Mr. Drop sat on his couch, turning page after page in Maggie's notebook. A loud ring startled him. He looked over at the phone on his desk, and something on the floor caught his eye. After turning the notebook upside down to save his place on the page, he walked over to the desk and picked up the paper. It was a letter he had written to his grandchildren in Zentobia.

He wrote letters to his family weekly since he had arrived in Hailsville. Even though he knew he had no way of getting the letters to them, he planned to share them with everyone upon his arrival home. *How had this letter fallen to the floor?* Several days had gone by since he had written to them last. Maggie and Peter must have snooped through his desk. Could he blame them, as he sat eagerly going through Maggie's notebook? He returned the letter to his desk and rushed back to the couch to resume his search.

CHAPTER SIX

The lights flickered on and off before the Millers' house went black. Griffen lit the candles, and he and Penny walked upstairs to say goodnight to the kids.

Maggie lifted her head from the desk at the sound of footsteps entering her room.

Her mom walked over and put a hand on her back. "I couldn't reach Mr. Drop. He might already be asleep."

"UGH, seriously? Who goes to sleep this early?" Tension built up in her mind as she took deep breaths, trying to calm down. *What if he reads the journal and finds out we followed him? I don't care if he sees my notes about the other cases, but what if he reads the entry where I talk about having a crush on Jackson? That would be so embarrassing! If he reads the stuff I wrote about the drama last week in English class, I will get in trouble for sure!*

"I'm sorry. We'll get it first thing in the morning when you see him. Try not to think about it and get some sleep." She kissed her on the forehead.

"Fine. I'll try, but it won't be easy."

"Um, Mom, Dad?" Peter beckoned from his room. "Can you come here? That is some crazy loud thunder."

The basketball memorabilia he had received on his last birthday kept him distracted from the storm. Memories of his old school's basketball team ran through his mind. His school in Hailsville didn't have a basketball team. It only had baseball, and he hated that sport. He thought about asking his gym teacher to organize a basketball team, but he kept chickening out.

His parents walked into his room.

"Jeez, you don't even need the candles, that lightning is so bright. This has got to be the biggest storm ever!"

"It's a good thing we're inside for the night," Dad said. "Hopefully, it will pass soon, and you can get some sleep."

"Yeah, yeah, oh, and by the way, I want to tell you guys something about Mr. Drop, but you have to promise you won't get mad." He walked over to his bed.

"How can we promise that if we don't know what it is?" his mom said. "But we can promise we'll never get mad when you tell the truth. So, go ahead, what is it?"

He thought this over carefully. *Should I tell them Mr. Drop told us he is from another world and risk them changing their mind about Maggie and me searching for the rainbow in the morning? Or, should I tell them about the papers with the strange writing and symbols in Mr. Drop's desk and see how they respond to that first? Maybe they will know something that could help explain his story. But will Dad be upset that we were sneaking around his living room after he told me not to snoop?*

Telling them about the odd writing and symbols seemed the safest choice.

"When we were at Mr. Drop's house, some random

papers were on the...floor, and strange writing and weird symbols covered them. I've never seen anything like it before." He didn't take a breath and hoped they wouldn't realize he'd lied.

His parents kept silent for a moment, which always worried him. Dad spoke up first. "These papers—were they written in cursive, maybe? You know some cursive writing can be hard to read."

"No, it definitely wasn't cursive. It was, uh, just different. And the symbols and drawings were strange, too. The only thing that looked normal was a rainbow on the page. I don't know what it is with this guy and rainbows. We're going to look for one in the morning. Who goes *rainbow hunting?*"

"Sounds like a fun idea to me," Mom said.

"Tell me more about the symbols and the rainbow on the papers," Dad said. The tone of his voice sounded like he was interviewing a suspect at the police station.

"They looked like lines, semi-circles, and circles put together in distinct ways, like puzzle pieces that didn't fit. Some kind of writing that didn't look like English was mixed in with the symbols. The rainbow just looked like the one on his wall."

As he spoke, another tremendous clap of thunder rang through the house. He jumped.

His dad put a hand on his shoulder. "I think we've all had a long day, and this storm is getting to us. Maybe it was a language that he studies. There are plenty of languages you are not familiar with. Or maybe someone gave him the papers, and he didn't write them. Perhaps on your walk you could ask him about it?"

He thought about this, but how would that work, unless he told Mr. Drop he went through his desk? "*Oh, hey, Mr.*

Drop, when I went through your desk without your permission yesterday, I saw some strange writing and symbols, and I really want to know what the heck it means." No way.

"Um, maybe." He averted his eyes. "We'll see how it goes. I just hope I wake up in time."

As his parents said goodnight, his mom glanced at the hallway window, and something seemed to catch her eye. "Look." She walked out of Peter's room and peered through the glass, straight into the living room window of Mr. Drop's home.

"Is it anything I need to see?" Peter called from his room. *I'm too tired.*

"No," Mom said. "It's Mr. Drop sitting at his desk, reading by candlelight. I thought he wasn't home when he didn't answer my call. But maybe his phone lines are down."

In Mr. Drop's living room, he made it halfway through Maggie's journal before his head drooped. A loud bang of thunder woke him up before he completely drifted off to sleep. His eyes opened wide, and a picture of the rainbow with the same setting that mirrored the one on his wall sat on the page before him. *Jackpot!*

CHAPTER SEVEN

Morning could not come soon enough for Mr. Drop. He spent half the night reading Maggie's notebook and the rest pondering her drawing of the rainbow. She drew hers in pencil, so it lacked the bright colors that adorned his painting, but it had an identical setting. There was no obvious start to it, but the end stood near several unusual rock formations. A small house sat behind a little hill with a tiny garden of flowers to its right. He vaguely recalled seeing a house behind a hill, but for the life of him, he couldn't remember where. *Maggie will help, and today is the day.*

He couldn't wait to get back home to see his family. He missed the long walks he and his wife took on the warm days in southern Zentobia. His heart ached to see his children and their families. He could picture the cheerful faces of his six grandchildren laughing as they cascaded down one of the town's floating waterfalls. The waterfalls separated the little villages that made up most of his side of the world, and the children slid down them for hours at a time. The former ruler of Zentobia, Mortis, had given Mr. Drop a home in the Crescent Village as a gift.

At seven fifty-five a.m., he collected Maggie's notebook and a bag before heading outside. He filled it with a daily newspaper, an automobile magazine, some of his favorite foods, and all the letters he had written to his family. He also stuffed it with the pair of flying shoes he'd worn when he arrived in Hailsville. Mostly, the items were to prove he had been in another world, since he feared no one at home would believe him. Plus, he found Earth's method of transportation fascinating and wanted to share it with others.

There were no automobiles in Zentobia. Zentobians got around from one place to another by walking or flying. Mr. Drop worked at a transport station that equipped Zentobians with special shoes that enabled them to fly. He worked in the shoe administration department, where he dispensed and retrieved the shoes from those who had to travel far distances or cross lakes and rivers. Boats were available for short distances, or it could take days to get from place to place. Zentobians could travel to the north side of the world in less than a day, but no one dared go there because they could be captured by the north's evil leader and become slaves.

At exactly eight a.m., Mr. Drop opened his front door. Maggie raced as fast as a dog chasing a ball toward his house. Peter and Bacon trailed behind.

"Good morning, Mr. Drop." She sprinted up to the door. "Did I leave my journal at your house last night?"

"Yes, you did, and I have it right here." He handed her the journal.

She started to hug him, but stopped. "Oh, phew!" She squeezed the journal close to her chest. "I was so worried I lost it. I wanted it for our adventure today. We brought

Bacon too. He hunts for more than just food, you know. If anyone can find that rainbow, Bacon can."

Mr. Drop eyed the dog and pulled out a dog treat he had tucked in his pocket.

"Here you go, Bacon." He put the treat in the dog's mouth. "Are you ready to go rainbow hunting and find the end of it? I know I am." He smiled from ear to ear.

The group headed down the street, looking up to the sky along the way.

After a few minutes of walking, Maggie nudged Peter and whispered, "Ask him about Zentobia." *I really want to know what he was talking about.*

"Why do I have to do it? You do it."

"No. You ask, and I'll write his answers down."

Peter threw up his hands. "Fine." He turned his gaze to Mr. Drop. "So...you mentioned something last night about wanting to go home to Zentobia? Is that a city somewhere?"

"It's not a city. It's another world. I know it might be hard for the two of you to believe, but like I said, I'm not from here." He stopped and faced them. "Once we find the rainbow's end, you'll see. I will finally be able to go home to my family."

"But if you have a painting of the rainbow on your wall, and you remember it, why do you need us to help you?" Maggie asked.

"I remember the rainbow, but I can't remember where it dropped me off. Every time I tried to follow the direction of it, I got lost. Maybe going through the portal did something to my memory."

Peter whispered to Maggie. "A portal? This is getting stranger by the minute."

"Shh. He'll hear you. Let's just go along and see what happens." Something above caught her attention. "There! There's a rainbow. Now we just have to follow it. I think I know where to go."

Mr. Drop's eyes glistened in the sunlight as the group trotted along toward the big, brightly colored arch in the sky.

CHAPTER EIGHT

M aggie's feet hurt from too much rainbow hunting. She could tell her sneakers were getting worn out, because the bottoms of her feet felt the little rocks poking through the shoes. *Definitely time for new ones.*

"What do you remember about where you saw the rainbow's end?" Mr. Drop asked Maggie.

"There were some weird rocks, and it was by a hill. Sorry, I don't remember anything else."

"Why don't you look for it in your notebook? I think we could all use a little break from walking."

She immediately stopped when she heard the word "break." Removing the weight of her backpack would help her feet too, she thought. After taking out her journal, she gave Peter a water bowl for Bacon. "Give Bacon some water while I look." She flipped through the pages for several minutes. "I found it! Look, I think this is it, and there's the hill and the strange rocks."

Peter glanced at the page. "Hey, I know where that is. That's right by Mr. Winter's house. You know, the mailman who hopes no one will find him when he delivers your mail to the wrong person's house. I hear he always blasts the horn when he comes home because he falls asleep and slumps over the steering wheel in his truck. I think he's getting old."

"Yikes!" Maggie giggled. "Good job on finding the location. How do we get there?"

Peter paused. "I think I know. Follow me."

Another fifteen minutes passed, and they found nothing.

"Do you know where you're going?" Mr. Drop asked impatiently. "It would be much easier if we just flew there."

Maggie and Peter broke out laughing.

"Fly there? That's impossible," Maggie said. "I know it's kind of a long walk, but you can only fly to other cities or states."

"In Zentobia we can fly with the help of special shoes." Mr. Drop continued to walk, waving his hands to usher them along.

"No way," Peter said, playing along. "I would like to try on a pair of those." His attention shifted up ahead. "Look, there's the hill. And we're right below the curve of the rainbow. Let's move closer."

Mr. Drop's casual walk turned into a sprint.

A strange rock formation caused Bacon to perk up and run ahead.

"That looks like the area I wrote about in my notebook," Maggie said. "I think this is it. Now what?"

"Now we just need to pinpoint the end," Mr. Drop said.

Maggie looked around carefully, as if she were trying to find the missing piece of a jigsaw puzzle.

Bacon's high-pitched barking caught everyone's attention.

"What has our nosy dog gotten himself into?" Peter

headed in that direction. "What the heck? I think Bacon found something! This way!"

The pooch's little paws were near a rainbow formation spewing from the ground. Maggie and Mr. Drop quickly made their way over.

"OMG, what are we looking at?" Peter stood as frozen as a popsicle. "Rays of light are coming out of the ground and floating right in front of us. How is this even possible? What kind of town did we move to?"

"I knew there was something strange about Hailsville," Maggie said. "I can't believe we are standing next to a real live rainbow!"

Peter knelt to get a better look. The bright beams caused his eyelids to close.

Maggie reached for her notebook to document their incredible discovery. She turned to Mr. Drop. "We found it!"

"Yes. We make a great team. Thank you very much for helping me. You two should probably get back home. And I need to go home too."

"No way! I have a lot to write, and we have more exploring to do here. Who knows what else we'll find? I wonder what happens if you touch it?" Maggie reached toward it.

"NO!" Mr. Drop yelled.

Maggie and Peter jumped back, and Bacon whimpered.

"I mean, I would be careful touching something unknown like this. What if it gives off an electrical shock?"

"I didn't learn that rainbows give off electrical current in any of the science classes I have taken," Peter said. "They are just lights. You can't touch them."

Peter slowly raised his hand toward the rainbow. As if in slow motion, his fingers carefully grazed the top of the rainbow and disappeared inside, like it had chopped them off. He pulled them out immediately.

"Um, what did I just see here?" Peter yanked his hand up to his face and inspected his fingers. "Did part of my fingers just disappear inside the rainbow?"

"Let me try!" Maggie slowly raised her fingers just as her brother did, getting the same result. "This is incredible. No one will ever believe it!"

Mr. Drop pointed in the opposite direction. "Um, where did Bacon go? Maybe you two should go find him. I think he's somewhere *way* over there."

Maggie and Peter ignored him. Peter pushed his hand into the rainbow, and it disappeared. He pulled it out as fast as he could.

"Maggie, you will not believe this. I felt something in there. Something pulled on my hand."

"Stop it. That's not possible." She assumed Peter was trying to trick her, like he always did. "I don't believe you. Watch me. I bet nothing will happen."

Maggie put her hand in the rainbow, and something pulled on it. She took it out faster than a tiny fish swimming away from a hungry shark. "Okay, that was strange." A quiet buzzing noise caused her to lean in closer. "Do you hear that noise? Where's it coming from?"

"Wait!" Mr. Drop yelped. "Don't go any further in that rainbow, or you'll never come out!"

Maggie and Peter scrunched their faces.

"Never coming out of a rainbow is not possible." Peter laughed. "I don't even think it's possible to go *inside* a rainbow, because it's not solid. I think our hands are just going through the lights. It's kind of like a cloud."

"But it *is* possible," Mr. Drop began, "because this

rainbow brought me to Hailsville. If you go inside, it will take you to Zentobia."

Maggie's jaw dropped. "We are going to need a little more proof that you are from another world."

"The strange lights coming out of the ground aren't proof enough?" Peter asked.

"Where I come from, there's a rainbow in the sky all year except for one day, when it rains. On my way to work, I noticed a strange break in the rainbow. When I went to investigate, I made the mistake of touching it. That's when it all happened."

Maggie let out her breath to ask, "What happened?"

"I heard a noise coming from inside the rainbow, so I stepped in to find out what it was. Something pulled me in deeper, and I got swept through a portal to Hailsville."

"This is all very hard to believe," Maggie said.

Mr. Drop opened his bag and pulled out a silver shoe with small wing-like flaps on each side. "This is a special shoe we wear in Zentobia that enables us to fly."

Peter moved closer to inspect the shoe. "Whoa...that is a fancy shoe. I have never seen anything like that. Can I touch it?"

"Yes," Mr. Drop said.

Maggie reached for it. "Okay, these shoes are unusual, that's for sure." *Maybe he is telling the truth.*

Mr. Drop put the shoe back in his bag. "Not only that, but the animals can talk."

Maggie giggled. "*Talking* animals?"

Before Mr. Drop could respond, the horn from Mr. Winter's mail truck blasted from behind the hill and startled Bacon. As the pup jumped, he knocked into Maggie, who fell forward into the rainbow. It happened so fast that she couldn't catch herself. The top half of her body vanished inside the rainbow, and the bottom half knelt outside of it on the ground.

"What's happening?" Peter gasped. "I can't see half her body. Maggie!"

She couldn't hear him. The inside of the rainbow fascinated her. The colors were intensely bright and bold, and she had to squint to see straight ahead. She moved around a little, careful not to go too far. But her curiosity got the best of her, and she brought the rest of her body inside the rainbow. Something tugged on her feet. Not a small tug like she'd felt earlier on her hand, but one that swept her feet out from under her. Screams for Peter left her mouth, but she didn't hear him answer. The tugging force grew stronger, and the low buzzing became louder. The force pulled her deeper into the rainbow until she lost consciousness and disappeared.

CHAPTER NINE

"Maggie!" Peter screamed. "Get out here. This is not funny! Where did she go?" He looked around frantically for Mr. Drop, but he wasn't there. "Mr. Drop? I could really use your help right now!"

His body trembled as he thought about doing the one thing he knew he had to do. He had to go inside the rainbow to find his sister. *This is way too scary. Is it going to hurt? What if I don't end up in the same place as Maggie? I just wanted to find a pot of gold at the end of the rainbow, not a portal to another world!*

He slowly put one shaky foot inside the rainbow, followed by the other, then stepped out as fast as he could before anything crazy happened. Mr. Drop appeared behind him.

"What the heck is happening, and where is my sister?" Peter asked. "That stuff you told us about Zentobia—I don't know if I believe it. But if it's true, what will happen when I go inside? Or can we wait right here for a minute and Maggie will come back? That would be a much better option."

"I don't know if she'll be able to come right back. I assume you'll travel to Zentobia where you can help her. We should both go now."

Peter moved closer to the rainbow and then stepped back. He muttered a few words of encouragement and placed both feet inside. *I can do this.* A low humming sound rang in his ears. He called eagerly for his sister. As he listened for an answer, a powerful tug swept his legs out from under him.

Could this really be happening? Before he knew it, he lost consciousness, and the force inside the rainbow swept him away.

Outside, Mr. Drop stood next to Bacon, about to enter the rainbow, when it disappeared.

"Wait! No! I need to go home! I need to find the children!"

He turned in a full circle. *Where did it go? I don't understand this! I missed my chance to get home by seconds!*

Tears welled in his eyes, and he slumped to the ground. He tried to calm the pounding inside his head, but it took over.

With a knot in his stomach, he knew what he had to do. Telling Griffen and Penny that he was from another world and had lost their children through a rainbow would not be easy. But maybe with Griffen's detective skills, they could find a way to bring back the portal.

CHAPTER TEN

The clunking sound of Mr. Drop's shoes dragging along the sidewalk cut through the muggy air as he walked up the street toward the Millers' house.

Bacon's barks echoed as he knocked faintly on the door. Penny opened it.

"Hello." She peered past him, looking for Maggie and Peter. "How was the day? Where are the kids?" The pup jumped down from Mr. Drop's arms and licked Penny's feet. "Is everything okay?"

"Can I come inside?" His feet moved as if ten-pound weights held them down. His eyes followed the floor. "I have a little story to tell you, but please don't be alarmed. Is Mr. Miller home?"

She bit her lip and beckoned. "Griffen! Come down here, please!"

Loud creaks coming from the stairs signaled Griffen's arrival.

"Mr. Drop was just about to tell us a story that will hopefully include the whereabouts of Maggie and Peter."

She clenched her jaw so tightly Mr. Drop thought she might break a tooth.

Griffen's eyebrows rose, and he glared at Mr. Drop. "What do you mean 'the whereabouts of Maggie and Peter?' Where are our kids?"

He'd rehearsed the speech the whole way to the Millers' house, but his mind went blank, and he couldn't form any words. *How will they ever believe me? This is a disaster.*

"What I am going to tell you might sound crazy, but please hear me out. First, your children are lovely, and I would never do anything intentionally to hurt them."

Griffen stepped closer. Mr. Drop took several steps back and tripped over his feet.

"Get to the point. Where are our kids?"

He fumbled over the words as they came spewing out of his mouth. "We went hunting for the rainbow's end, and upon finding it, we found a...a...portal to another... um...world. The kids, well, they, um....um...they jumped into the portal, and I can only assume it transported them to Zentobia."

A high-pitched shriek escaped Penny's mouth. "What are you even talking about? Tell me where my kids are!"

Griffen put a hand on her shoulder.

Mr. Drop explained how he had arrived in Hailsville. "The rain was coming down that day, which was unusual. After I reached the rainbow's end, I encountered thin brown grass, limp plants, and broken stems from flowers scattered all over. I'm afraid the south side of my world was beginning to die. When I approached the rainbow, I could step inside it, but then a powerful force pulled me deeper, and I lost consciousness. The next thing I knew, I woke up here."

"This story is ridiculous. I want to see my children

now!" Penny got her phone and dialed Peter's number. "Peter's not answering his phone. What have you done with them?"

The flame in Griffen's eyes could have lit a torch. He motioned for Mr. Drop to take a seat at the kitchen table. "I should remind you that I'm a detective at the police department, so if you're trying to pull something here, it will not work. If it's money you want, we don't have any. I highly advise you to turn over our kids now."

"Money? No, I don't want money or anything. I told you what happened. I wish I could get them back, but we must wait for the portal to appear again, or perhaps, with your detective skills, we can find it." He lowered his head, his body shriveling up in the chair.

"Stay here," Griffen said to Mr. Drop. He gestured for Penny to follow him into the other room.

"What the heck is going on here?" she asked. Her body shivered. "A *being* from another world? A rainbow that sends people through a portal? I just want to see the kids!"

Griffen wrapped his arms around her as tears dripped down her cheeks. *How am I going to explain this to her?* "I know this all sounds crazy, but I have something to tell you. There have been some strange happenings around town. I've been helping the sheriff try to figure things out."

She pushed him away. Her eyes widened. "What do you mean 'strange happenings,' and what does this have to do with finding our children?"

"Listen to me carefully," he began. "People have gone missing recently. Some officers found soil dug up in random places around town, and there have been reports of unidentified people in Hailsville following rainbows. They spotted one at what the officer described as rays of light coming out of the ground. I arrived at an empty location when he brought me back to check out the scene. McCall put together a special team to investigate the missing people. It was a bunch of dead ends. They've also been trying to keep tabs on these unknown people, and Mr. Drop is one of them. Leaving the kids with him didn't worry me because I've gotten to know him a little, and nothing turned up suspicious about him. Until now. I'm not saying I believe this guy, but I'm not dismissing his story either."

Penny's legs buckled, and Griffen caught her. "What the heck, Griffen? You didn't think it was important enough to tell me that our neighbor is on the sheriff's watch list? I couldn't figure out why you wanted to take a job in a town that no one's ever heard of, but if it's full of missing people and supernatural happenings, then that would explain it. It would have been nice to know that before I agreed to move here, and before I agreed to let the kids hang out with this man. Do you believe he's some kind of creature from another world?"

"I don't know what to believe. From what I've experienced, this thing coming out of the ground doesn't stick around long enough for anyone to examine it. An officer will spot it, call me to investigate, but it disappears before I get there. If Drop is telling the truth, then maybe he could help put these pieces together. What I know is, we need to find out more about him and more about this town. He needs to take us to where he went with the kids. Now."

They walked back to the kitchen. Mr. Drop sat with Bacon curled up in his lap.

"I need you to tell me every detail about your time

today with Maggie and Peter," Griffen said. "Start from the beginning and leave nothing out."

Mr. Drop shared all the details of the visit with Griffen. Shallow heaving came from his lungs as he replayed the day's events. "The last place I saw the kids was at the rainbow's end."

"Then we have to go there now." Griffen walked over to the door. "Let's find this portal."

CHAPTER ELEVEN

Maggie opened her heavy eyes in Zentobia, straining to focus and make sense of what had just happened. She tried to sit up, but the weight of her spinning head pulled her down. Familiar whining nearby startled her.

"Peter, is that you?" She pushed herself up. Droplets the color of oranges fell all around her. *Is this rain?* Her eyes could barely see through the far-reaching fields of grass and tall, lush trees. Her nose itched from too much pollen and the abundance of aromatic flowers. The high-pitched sound of birds chirping made the buzzing in her ears even louder. Peter's moaning directed her to his location a few feet away under a tree. She stood, grabbed her backpack, and slowly made her way over to him.

"Are you okay?" She opened her bag and reached for her journal.

"You have got to be kidding me," Peter groaned, trying to sit up. "We just landed smack in the middle of who-knows-where and you go straight for your notebook. How about we figure out where the heck we are first before you take notes like we're on a case?"

She ignored him. "Look at this place. I think we traveled to another world through a rainbow! This is the biggest case of our lives." Maggie flipped open her notebook and wrote about the colored rain. "And, if you haven't noticed, the rain is orange."

Peter looked up and extended his hands to catch the falling drops. "What if this isn't rain?" He touched his head and examined the clear water covering his fingertips. "Wait...it's coming down orange but then turns clear." The rain stopped. "It's disappearing. This is weird and cool."

Maggie wrote about the vanishing rain until a squeaking sound caught her attention. Mr. Drop's den of animals came to life right in front of her, times ten. Bunnies ran across fields, butterflies fluttered in droves, and little squirrels scurried about. Unless her eyes were playing tricks on her, it looked like two of the squirrels were having a conversation.

"I think I see two squirrels fighting over an acorn." Peter scanned the area. "Where is Mr. Drop? He said he would come with me. He can tell us how to get home."

"I just thought of something. What if he didn't make it through the rainbow? He said he's been stuck in Hailsville." Her throat tightened, not letting any air through until she forced herself to breathe. "Wait...what if we're stuck in Zentobia?"

A solid red bird with yellow spots landed right at her feet, chirping rapidly. She jumped back, turned the page in her notebook, and wrote about the bird.

Peter's hands flew into the air and over his face. "We don't have time for that! We might be trapped here, and there is a bird as red as a lobster aggressively chirping at your feet. And speaking of lobster, I'm starving. You know it's about lunchtime right now."

"I know, but if we *are* stuck here and Mr. Drop didn't make it back, we should at least find his family and let them know he's okay. And we have to figure out how to get home."

"Oh, that's all we have to do?" He sounded hysterical. "How do you think we'll accomplish all that when we don't even know if we *are* in his world? We don't know where we are, and I'm not sure I want to find out."

The sound of children laughing interrupted their banter. Maggie shifted her gaze in the direction of the noise.

"Whoa...Peter, look at that." She pointed to large waterfalls floating above-ground. "Those kids are sliding down waterfalls that aren't attached to anything. How is that possible? I want to do that!" A group of kids were in a line, coasting to the top of where one waterfall started. The water fell straight into a pool on the ground. "How are they getting to the top of that? There are no steps."

"At least not ones we can see from this far away," Peter said.

"We should go investigate. And that might involve trying it ourselves."

"What? I don't know if that's a good idea. Maybe we should find our way home before it gets too late."

Maggie put on her backpack and headed to the waterfalls. "I think we should check it out for just a few minutes first. Come on...let's go!" Her fast-paced walk turned into a sprint, and Peter raced to catch up.

They weaved between a cluster of little homes slightly elevated from the ground.

Maggie stopped in front of a yellow house that looked like it was made of clay. "Wow! Can you imagine living in something that floats in the air? And it's so small and cute, like a cottage in a fairytale. What if Mr. Drop's family lives around here? We should survey the area and ask the people that live here some questions."

"No. This is not the right time for playing detective. We need to stay out of sight. Not everyone is as friendly as Mr. Drop. We don't know anything about this place yet."

"Then it's a good thing we're out exploring. Look! Up ahead. I bet that will be the funnest water slide we've ever done."

"It does look cool. Okay, follow my lead. Just act like we belong."

Maggie looked down at her clothes. "Uh, Peter? That might not be too believable. We don't have bathing suits."

"Oh, yeah, right. If anyone asks, we can say they're in the wash or something."

Maggie grinned. "Good idea. Let's go."

Peter took off in the waterfall's direction.

As they got closer, the vision of a line of kids moving upward to reach the top of the slide came into Maggie's view. "How are they getting to the top? It looks like they are going up an escalator, but I don't see one."

"Only one way to find out."

Peter got in line, and Maggie followed. Each child ahead placed a foot in front of them to reveal a single step that carried them to the top. Once they headed upward, the step disappeared.

"Do you see that?" Maggie asked.

"I see it, and I'm a little nervous to try it. But I'll go first." Peter inched his way to the front of the line.

The kids behind them whispered and stared. Maggie folded her arms and looked down.

Please don't let them ask questions.

Peter stepped up to go next. He placed one foot out, and a wide, gold step appeared. Once he positioned himself on it, it slowly glided him to the top.

Maggie's breath quickened at the sight of how high she had to go to reach the start of the slide. Peter's joyful screams going down eased her nerves. *Peter is a much bigger chicken than I am, so if he is having fun, then I know I can do this.*

"What are you waiting for? It's your turn," a child behind her said.

Maggie turned and smiled. "Oh, sorry. I wasn't paying attention." She moved forward and put out her foot. The gold step appeared.

On her way to the top, she heard Peter yelling from below, "Maggie, it's so much fun. I'll meet you at the bottom."

With her hands waving wildly in the air, she flew down the slide faster than Bacon chasing his ball. "Whoooaaa!"

Peter met her when she stepped out of the small pool of waves at the bottom. "This is the best slide I have ever been on. I think we should do it a couple more times."

Maggie agreed, and they ran to the back of the line. After two more times up and down the slide, they moved away from the waterfall to wring out their clothes.

The red bird that had greeted them when they first arrived in Zentobia appeared again, chirping at Maggie's feet.

"I think that's the same bird we saw earlier," Maggie said. "How weird it's here again."

The bird's chirping grew louder and faster.

"I think this bird is trying to tell us something. Mr. Drop said the animals in his world can talk. Maybe this is one of them." She bent over and lowered her head toward the bird to listen.

Peter rolled his eyes just as the bird walked away. Its little feet moved quicker than expected, and it looked back at them every few steps.

"Well, that's kind of creepy." Peter stared at the bird.

"Come on, let's follow it." She moved to catch up. "It might lead us to a clue."

"NO! We are not going to follow a bird! Let's head this way. I think we should try to find the rainbow's end and see if it will take us home."

Maggie ignored him. She took off in the other direction, following close behind the bird.

CHAPTER TWELVE

As Penny, Griffen, and Mr. Drop approached the rainbow's end, Griffen surveyed the area. "This is close to where Mr. Winter, the mailman, lives."

"Yes, he's kind of responsible for setting this entire thing in motion. As I mentioned before, he fell asleep in his truck, and his face landed on the horn, which made Bacon jump and accidentally push Maggie into the rainbow."

"That's a heck of a story. I will speak to Mr. Winter to see exactly where he was at the time this happened. Now, where is this..." He stopped in his tracks and put an arm in front of Penny's chest. The sight of glowing rays of light coming out of the ground knocked him off balance. "No one move. What the heck am I looking at, Drop?"

"Just like I told you. It's the rainbow's end."

As soon as Griffen removed his hand from Penny's chest, she sprinted closer to it. "Am I actually seeing the end of a rainbow? It looks like some kind of shiny foreign object, but that's impossible. I still don't understand why...I mean...how did the kids go into this? How can we get them back from here?" She ran her hands over the colorful arch.

Griffen grabbed her hand, squeezing it tight. He slowly put out his fingers to touch it, and they brushed through it. He took out his phone and captured a photograph.

"You said the kids went through a portal? How did that happen? Is there a door?" Griffen asked. "I want to go through this thing now to get the kids." Griffen put his foot inside the rainbow, and the colors faded around him.

"It's disappearing!" Penny said.

"This happened when I tried to go after the kids. The rainbow faded before I could go through it," Mr. Drop said.

Tears escaped Penny's eyes. "No! How can we get it back?"

"Maybe it has to do with the rain," Mr. Drop said.

"The rain?" Griffen asked, remembering the areas of town with the soil dug up.

"The day after the yearly rainstorm in Zentobia is when I went through the rainbow. So, I've been searching for the rainbow's end after it rains to see if I can replicate what brought me here."

Griffen wondered if, since Mr. Drop was searching for the rainbow's end to get home, other people from Zentobia could be in Hailsville looking for the same thing. "I need you to be honest with me. Are there other people from your world in Hailsville?"

Mr. Drop cocked his head. "I don't know. But if I passed through the rainbow, I am sure others could have too."

Griffen's mind raced as the pieces came together. *Could the missing people from Hailsville have gone through the rainbow by accident?*

"We've found areas around town with soil dug up. If you had other people from your...um—I can't believe I am saying this, *your world*—here in Hailsville, would they have any reason to dig up the soil?"

Mr. Drop raised his brows. "The land in half of our world, the north side, has died, and I mentioned earlier about the south. Perhaps they are bringing back something from the soil to help revive the ground to save it."

Griffen lowered his head. The thought of beings from another world coming to Hailsville to steal minerals from the soil to save their world seemed absurd. But with what he had just witnessed and his kids missing, it might not be that far-fetched.

"I think we need to head to the police station and talk to Sheriff McCall. I'll check the weather forecast to find out when it will rain next. I don't know if your rain theory is correct, but it's worth a try. It might be the only chance we have to find Maggie and Peter."

CHAPTER THIRTEEN

Peter's legs ached as he raced to catch up to Maggie, who was following the red bird. It sprinted so fast his sneakers were the only thing helping him keep up.

"Maggie!" he called. "Slow down! Why are you following this bird when I told you we need to find our way back home?"

She slowed her pace and turned to him. "This bird is taking us somewhere, and maybe if we follow it, we can get some answers. Don't you want to know where we are and find out how to get home?"

Peter shrugged. On one hand, he wanted to know where they were. But what if this bird was leading them farther away from the rainbow and they got lost forever?

Rustling sounds above interrupted his train of thought.

"Maggie! Look up! I can't believe what I'm seeing. Those people are flying! Wait, there's so many. There's..." He counted them. "Six people flying over our heads!"

Silver flames escaped the bottom of the elongated shoes worn by the figures above. They weaved through the air like children going through a maze. Two of them hovered in place, their feet held steady and their bodies balanced as if they were standing on solid ground.

Maggie stared up at the sky. "That's amazing! Look at them go!" She grabbed her brother's arm. "Do you remember when we were searching for the rainbow with Mr. Drop and he said it would be easier to fly there? And then he showed us those special shoes? He was being serious."

Before Peter could get out another word, the bird stopped at a small, nondescript, white building with no visible windows and a single brown door.

"Maybe the bird wants us to go inside." She placed her hand on the doorknob.

"No way." He pushed her hand away. "Do *not* open that door. We don't know what's inside. What if it's a trap?"

A faint whisper came from below. "Go inside."

"Did you just hear that?" She brushed her hands over her arms. "The bird—it talked! I have goosebumps."

"Yep. I'm speechless right now."

"That never happens. I better write this down."

The bird said again, "Go inside."

Before Peter could stop her, Maggie opened the door. She peered inside and took baby steps forward. He followed. A loud boom from behind made them jump.

"I knew it!" He turned and tried to open the door. "This was a trap! We got trapped in a room by a talking bird! How stupid are we? This is all your fault!"

Tears welled up in her eyes. As she moved haphazardly around the dark room, her shoes left a trail of footprints behind from the piles of dust. She bumped into one of several scattered, rickety wooden chairs.

Peter ran to a door in the back of the room, but it wouldn't open. He pulled on it fruitlessly and hit it with his fists, yelling for anyone to let them out. But no one heard his cries.

"I'm sorry!" She took out her journal and pen from her backpack and slid into the wobbly chair. It delivered a layer of dust that covered her pants.

"Is that your response to this disaster?" Peter asked. "While you're trying to solve this case by writing, I'll be looking for a way out of here. It would be faster if you helped me."

Peter explored the room, searching for anything that might help them escape. A small, round, dark table positioned in the center held flickering candles that cast a shallow glow. Several paintings of unfamiliar people hung on the walls, covered in dust. A shaggy rug lay on the ground by the back door. Nothing filled the rest of the room. *There has got to be a way out of here!*

CHAPTER FOURTEEN

Peter couldn't find anything to help them get out of the locked room. He stopped to rest.

Shuffling noises signaled someone's—or something's—approach.

Maggie quickly put her notebook in her backpack and ran next to him as the door in the back of the room opened. She squeezed his hand so hard, the sound of his knuckles cracking pierced through the room.

A beautifully-dressed woman with cascading brown hair as shiny as silk walked inside. The little red-and-yellow bird that had trapped them in the room and a bulky black dog followed by her side.

That dog hasn't missed a meal, Peter thought.

The woman moved closer, her shoes thumping against the wood floor. "I am Minka, leader of the south side of Zentobia. I would welcome you, but I don't yet know if you are welcome. Did Cyrus send you? Are you from the north side of the world?"

"Um...look, we are not here to do any harm," Peter said. "I'm Peter, and this is my sister Maggie. We don't know anyone named Cyrus. We don't even know where we are. We just want to go home."

"If that is true, then how did you get here?" Minka said. "No outsider has ever been to this side of the world before, and we don't dare go to the north. Some not-so-friendly Zentobians and animals that lost their way live in the north side of the world."

Maggie jumped in. "If we tell you how we got here, will you help us get home and find our friend's family and tell them he's okay? I think someone from your world is in ours, and he's been trying to get back here for a long time."

"You are from another world?" Minka leaned closer. "Tell me more about your friend."

"Sure, that's Mr. Drop. And, yes, we are from Earth and live in a boring town called Hailsville."

Minka's eyes widened.

Maggie spilled the entire story about Mr. Drop, how they found the end of the rainbow that transported them to Zentobia, and how their neighbor was stuck behind.

The little bird chirped frantically.

"That's quite a story," Minka said. "We had a man who disappeared a little while ago, and no one ever found him. But his name wasn't Mr. Drop. It was Mr. Walric."

"It has to be the same person. How many people disappear through a rainbow portal? Do you know about it?" Peter asked. "Can it get us back home?"

The bird tilted her head and tweeted at the kids. Minka put her hand over the bird's beak.

"I think your bird is trying to tell us something," Peter said. "I thought I heard her speak actual words when she coaxed us to enter this room."

"Yes, Talia can speak when she wants to. But I need to be sure you are telling the truth."

"How could we possibly make any of this stuff up?"

"You seem to know quite a bit about the rainbow." Minka studied them for a moment.

"That's because we went through it. But we really don't know anything about Zentobia," Maggie said.

"My side of the world is in danger. Cyrus, the leader of the north, wants to take over the south. When I learned of your arrival, I thought he sent you here to wreak havoc. But I can see that is not the case. I will help you."

Hope rose within Peter. "Thank you."

"Have a seat. Chester will bring you something to eat and drink." Minka gave a hand signal to the dog to retrieve food and drinks from the pantry. The chunky mutt trotted off.

"Why does Cyrus want to control the south?" Maggie asked.

Minka's expression resembled a teacher in a classroom getting ready to give a history lesson. "Because he wants more power. Many years ago, Cyrus and I reached an understanding that he would stay in his part of the world and not expand his power into the south. But he broke that agreement and has been controlling the weather by making it rain here more than it's supposed to. The rain damages the rainbow and causes the soil to die. Fortunately, we found a way to stop the soil from dying," she said. "One day when it rained, a bird discovered the portal inside the rainbow that leads to your world. Cyrus didn't know that the excess rain would open a portal. The bird went through it and came back with wet soil on his feet. When he walked through Zentobia, the dying ground where he stepped came back to life. We determined the minerals in the wet soil were saving our land. So, our people go to Hailsville to collect the soil and bring it back here to test and stockpile."

"Wow, this is incredible!" Maggie reached for her notebook. "Our town is saving your world! Do you mind if I write all this down? This will make history!"

Peter grabbed her hand before she could open the journal. "Not now."

She reluctantly put it down. "If people from your world have been coming over to ours, why couldn't Mr. Drop—I mean—Mr. Walric, get back?"

"When our people go to your world, they have to drink something special beforehand so their memory will stay intact. If Mr. Walric didn't drink the elixir, he could have become disoriented. But worse, he would have no idea how to find the portal again."

"That would explain all the rainbow hunting," Peter said. "How come no one in Hailsville noticed random people digging up soil?"

Before she could answer, a squealing Chester sprinted through the door, rolling a squeaky cart covered with food and drinks.

Peter's stomach rumbled as he eyed a buffet of unfamiliar cuisine. Steam rose from trays overflowing with fluffy white breads and bowls full of colorful, solid bites. He scrunched up his nose, trying to identify the various smells that reminded him of pizza and homemade chocolate- chip cookies.

Peter and Maggie stood still.

Minka reached for a plate. "This is a sample of our favorite foods. If I were you, I would try the dresdle and the tigwat." She pointed to each item.

Maggie grabbed a plate first and scooped up what Minka had suggested. Peter followed.

"The dresdle tastes like macaroni and cheese," Maggie

said to Peter as she swallowed a small bite of the creamy, soup-like concoction.

He nodded, mouth overflowing with warm dresdle.

She went for the tigwat next. Her teeth crunched into the small, round, fuzzy piece of fruit. "The tigwat is delicious. It looks like a peach but tastes like chocolate candy. I think it's my new favorite food. This is so weird to be eating food from another world."

"It comes from the Tigwat tree," Minka said. "The trees are all over this side of the world. But they could disappear if our soil dies. The people in Hailsville are noticing their soil is being dug up. We think your police followed several of our people."

Peter gagged on the tigwat stuffed in his mouth. "Did you say police? Our dad is with the police."

CHAPTER FIFTEEN

The Hailsville Police Department didn't see much unusual activity. Aside from an occasional speeding ticket, neighborhood disturbance, or shoplifting case, crime was low, and the tight-knit group of officers prided themselves on that. When Sheriff McCall formed the secret task force a year ago to investigate the missing people and observe the ones following the rainbow, the officers were happy to have something new to do. But the task force came up empty-handed. That was when McCall brought in a skilled detective, Griffen Miller, to help shed new light on the investigation.

Griffen, Penny, and Mr. Drop walked into the police station, which smelled of old sneakers and coffee. They headed straight to Griffen's work station. A computer keyboard barely peeked through the papers scattered across his desk. He gestured for them to have a seat and headed toward McCall's office. As he approached, McCall waved him inside.

"Griffen, what can I do for you?" McCall paced the room. "Anything new with the investigation?"

"Yes, actually, I have a lot of fresh information for you. I think you might want to have a seat for this one." He went through the day's events.

When he finished his briefing, he slumped into a chair and waited for his boss's reply.

"Holy cow. I don't even know what to say to all of this. It's a hard story to swallow. Are you sure Drop doesn't have your kids stashed somewhere, or they didn't run off? I put him up in my rental house because he was wandering around like he had nowhere to go, and I felt sorry for the guy. And I like to keep an eye on any newbies to town. I never pegged the man to come up with a story like this."

"I know, I know. I wouldn't believe it either if I didn't see the rainbow's end myself." He showed him the photo he had taken at the site. McCall's mouth dropped. "My kids wouldn't run off, but they *would* run through a portal to another world."

McCall glued his eyes to the photo. "Is that for real? You didn't doctor up something to trick me?"

Tension built in Griffen's mind. "No. These are my kids we're talking about."

"So, you're telling me that what we have here in Hailsville is something coming out of the ground that links to another world? When the other guys on the task force told me they saw it, I didn't believe them, because they couldn't produce any proof. They said it always disappeared before they could take a stinkin' photo!"

"They probably tried, but this thing vanishes fast."

"You know what this is, don't you?" Beads of sweat dripped from his brows. "We've got a *major* discovery, Griffen."

"Yeah...I know. But we can figure all that out later. I just want to get my kids back."

"We can do both at the same time. You find your kids, and I'll handle the rest. I want to know what the heck is happening in Hailsville. I'll need some solid proof about this other world. Is Drop with you? Maybe he knows what happened to the people here that went missing. I want to talk to that guy."

"Yeah. I'll send him in when I leave. Let me know if you find out anything new. I'm going to go check the weather forecast, since the opening of the portal might be tied into the rain somehow."

"No need to check it. We're bracing for another big storm tonight. Already have extra patrol scheduled to monitor the roads. It's going to be a big one. Sounds like the perfect time for this rainbow portal to open again."

CHAPTER SIXTEEN

"Your father works for the police in Hailsville?" Minka asked Maggie and Peter.

Ugh, why did Peter have to tell Minka that? Maggie looked at Peter, about to retract what he said, when Peter spoke first.

"Yes, he's a detective. But there's no way he knows anything about this world." Peter wiped his sweaty palms on his jeans. "He would have told us."

"I am afraid you won't be going anywhere for a while. Now that you have discovered our world and what we're doing, it's too dangerous to send you back until we can come up with a plan. I'm sorry. Chester will make arrangements for you to stay in my palace until further notice."

Maggie's face turned as white as a blank page in her journal. She looked at Peter and knew he was daydreaming about staying in a palace.

"But what about Mr. Walric and his family? And our family?" Maggie asked. "They will wonder what happened to us. We have to go home!"

Minka and Talia left the room without answering,

leaving Chester behind. "Get your stuff together and follow me," the dog ordered.

"Did you just hear what I heard?" Peter walked closer to Chester and touched the chunky animal's head. "The dog talked. It didn't bark. It didn't growl. It talked!"

"Yep, I heard it. Just like we heard the bird," Maggie said, annoyed. "Look, Chester, I know you have orders to take us to the palace, which I would really like to see, but we need to get back to the rainbow and get home. Can you help us?"

Chester's tail sank between his legs, and his nose scraped the ground. She could tell he would be of no help. They would have to escape. She nudged Peter as he swallowed one last slurp of dresdle.

"Is there a bathroom we can use?' She grabbed her backpack and winked at Peter. Chester looked like food could easily distract him. "My brother and I need to go. Feel free to eat the rest of our food while we're gone."

Chester eyed the food and waved his paw in the direction of the bathroom.

As soon as he started chomping on the leftovers, Maggie whispered, "This way."

"But the bathroom is that way. And I have to go."

"No time, big brother. We're getting out of here. I only said we had to go to the bathroom to distract Chester so we could escape. I thought Minka would help us, but as soon as you told her Dad is with the police, she changed her mind. I don't think we can trust her."

"I didn't know that would happen. But you might be right. As much as I would love to stay and meet more talking animals, I would rather come back when there is not a war going on between the north and south sides of the world."

They ran down the narrow hall and opened a door that led to the outside.

"How long do you think it will take Chester to realize we're not coming back?" Peter asked.

"There wasn't too much food left, so not that long. Which way do we go? Everything looks the same."

They stopped to take in the surroundings. The blotchy tigwats hanging from the trees looked like tennis balls covered in mud after a big rainstorm in Hailsville. Maggie put her hands over her ears from the high-pitched sound of birds chirping in every direction.

"It looks like we're in a house of mirrors. I think we should head this way," Peter said. "No, that way...Okay, if we try to retrace our steps, we probably came from the south, so we should head north."

"That makes no sense. Not to mention, we don't want to go anywhere near the north end of this world, based on what Minka said. But we need to go now, before Chester comes charging out here. I think it's this way. Let's go."

They navigated through dense trees and tall shrubs, looking behind them every few steps for the dog, hoping he wasn't on their trail. They picked up their pace.

After what seemed like hours, Maggie stopped to catch her breath. "I can't go anymore. I need a break."

"Fine, but make it a fast one." Peter scoured the empty sky. There were no butterflies fluttering, birds chirping, or animals scuffling about. "Um, I'm getting a strange feeling. Why is it getting dark outside? It's not even night yet."

"You always have strange feelings. Maybe it's just overcast." She grabbed her backpack. "I'm ready. Let's go." They moved quickly, heading straight for the north side of the world.

CHAPTER SEVENTEEN

As day transitioned into night in Zentobia, Maggie and Peter had already covered a lot of ground. A sharp pain shot through Maggie's leg, and she bent over to grab it with weak hands. They stopped next to a tall tree and sat down to catch their breaths. Dead grass surrounded them, and the weathered tree didn't have any leaves.

"We haven't seen anything in forever. We're lost!" Peter sounded like he was about to cry. "We should have turned around way back there. Now we're who-knows-where, and it's getting dark."

Maggie reached for her notebook. She flipped through the last few pages and nodded. "Yep, you're right. This is not the same place where the rainbow dropped us off. There were butterflies and flowers and animals running all over. Right now, I only see..." She looked around. "Brown grass and trees without leaves. And, OMG, look up! There are five things in the sky that look like stars, but they are dark and spooky looking. Um...I have to tell you something."

Her breathing sped up. She realized they might no

longer be in the south side of the world. A scuffling noise from above prevented her from telling Peter.

"Quick, follow me." Peter pulled her wrist, and they ran behind the tree and into a big ditch. They crouched as low as they could and covered their heads with nearby branches. A group of scraggly brown-and-gray owls landed in front of the tree.

"It's a bunch of owls!" she said. "They look so cute. Maybe we should ask them where we are."

"No! Remember, the animals in the north are not nice. If we are in the north, then who knows what they will do? Maybe they'll eat us!"

Maggie didn't want to get eaten by an owl, so she stopped talking.

The owls scattered. Half went one way, and the others went the opposite, as if they were splitting up to search for their prey.

"Don't make a sound. Maybe they won't come back," Peter whispered.

After scouring the area, the owls gathered in front of the tree, chatting rapidly back and forth.

"What could they possibly be talking about?" she asked.

"Shh!" Peter's foot accidentally broke a branch. A loud crackle echoed from below his shoe. He stood motionless.

After several minutes, the owls all flew away, their wings waving uncontrollably in the sky.

"That was close. Let's go back the way we came." Heaps of oxygen escaped from Peter's lungs.

They jumped out of the ditch and headed the other direction.

Within a matter of seconds, dozens of owls swooped down and cut them off. Maggie jumped so far back she almost fell over. Peter grabbed her arm and caught her.

"Well, well, well, what do we have here?" one owl said. They all glared at the kids. "Looks like we have some new visitors, boys. Why don't we make them feel welcome?"

She didn't feel welcome. Not at all. She really regretted leaving Chester now.

"Maggie, let's run back in the other direction. Go! Now!" Peter said.

They took off running. Peter led by a few feet.

A tall, unnervingly thin man swallowed by a dark, over-sized cape floated down from the sky with two uniformed guards by his side. They landed between Maggie and Peter. The guards grabbed Maggie and held her in place. She struggled to break free, but their grip was too tight.

"Peter!"

His eyes locked with Maggie's.

"Keep running. Go get help!" she screamed.

He hesitated for a moment, then raced back to the south to find Minka, his tall frame fading in the distance.

"Well now, I was hoping to avoid that, but at least we have one of you," Cyrus said, waving his cape across his frail, wrinkled face. His sunken eyes barely peered through a mane of messy hair the color of slick black paint dotted with silver specks. "Perhaps you are tired of the south side of the world and have come to join us here? Unless that is not the case?"

Maggie's heart beat faster than Talia's frantic chirping. She didn't know whether to lie and say she wanted to move to the north side of the world, pretend she was lost, or tell the truth. The man's creepy mannerisms scared her. His slithering fingers didn't stop moving, and they darted to and from a knife hanging from his belt. She didn't want to find out what would happen if he found out she was lying.

Hypnotized by his dancing hands, she snapped out of it

and blurted, "I'm lost! But I think I just figured out which way to go, so I can be on my way now." She wiggled to get out of the guard's grip.

"Not so fast. I am Cyrus. Now that we've met, we should get to know each other. You are much younger than any of my previous visitors. Are you hungry? Why don't we head back to my...err...residence and I can give you some dinner? Screech, my head owl, and his friends will escort you. It's not far."

"Thank you, but no thank you. I'm expected home. I'm late, and my parents are out looking for me."

"I don't think you understood. It wasn't a yes or no question. We'll head back this way now, and then you can tell me all about home and where you come from. I haven't had much luck getting information from the other newcomers. But I have a good feeling that's about to change."

"My brother is going to come back for me, you know. He'll have people with him."

Cyrus laughed. "That's what they all say."

"Follow me and don't try any funny stuff," Screech said. "There's a lot of hungry animals out there at this time of day, and they will do anything to get their dinner. See you back at the palace, Cyrus."

A haunting grin grew across Cyrus's pale face. He and his guards flew off in the direction of his palace, farther and farther away from the south side of the world.

CHAPTER EIGHTEEN

The intense storm kept much of Hailsville awake most of the night, including Griffen. He stood at his kitchen table stuffing flashlights, ropes, flare guns, a compass, and other small essentials tightly into a backpack.

Penny walked over to the dog food and scooped out a few cups. "Here you go, Bacon. We might be gone for a few days, so I'm going to leave you a hearty helping of food. Aunt Stella will come over several times a day to check on you and let you outside." She turned to Griffen. "Looks like you're bringing quite a bit of firepower."

"It's not that much. I wish I had more. I don't know where we're going or what to expect when we get there. I just hope we won't need to use any of this to get the kids back."

The doorbell rang, and Penny jumped.

Griffen put a hand on her shoulder. "It's okay. That must be Drop. You ready?"

She nodded.

Griffen opened the door and waved his neighbor inside. Bacon immediately ran over and jumped for attention. Mr.

Drop took a dog treat out of his pocket and set it on the floor for the pup to enjoy.

"I see there is a rainbow," Mr. Drop said. "Ready to go?"

Griffen grabbed his backpack, and the three headed out. No one spoke on the way there. The sound of a cell phone ringing broke the silence.

"Sheriff, you got my message? I sent you the coordinates this morning. We're just about to approach the location. If we're not back in three days, we'll be expecting that rescue as soon as someone can make it through the portal...Okay... Got it...Thanks."

"Three days?" Penny said. "I was hoping we would be home by dinner."

He smiled reassuringly. The spot where Mr. Drop had taken them on the day the kids disappeared came into view.

Mr. Drop bolted to the rainbow's end. "It's here! We should be able to make it through! I'll go first, and you two follow. Move in fast before it disappears and the portal closes. If we get separated, remember, the rainbow in Zentobia is between the north and south parts of the world, so head south. Do *not* go north."

"How am I supposed to know which way is north and south? Will a compass work?" Griffen asked.

"I don't know what a compass is. Look for the gold star in the sky and head that direction." He slid his hand through the bottom of the rainbow and then stepped inside. Several seconds went by, and he didn't reappear.

"Did you see that?" Penny leaned her head closer. "He's gone! He didn't come out of the lights!"

Griffen stepped forward, keeping in mind they had to move fast. "This is all the proof I need that our kids did the same thing, and maybe even the people who went missing. We have to leave now. As soon as I go, follow behind me, and we'll meet on the other side. If we get separated, remember what he said about the gold star."

He kissed her forehead and hugged her tightly. She kept her arms around him longer than she should have, because the colors were fading.

"Look! You have to go now! If I don't make it, find the kids and bring them back!"

He didn't hesitate and leaped into the rainbow. A loud buzz rang in his ears, and a forceful tug swept his feet out from under him. He screamed for her to join him, but he didn't hear a response. Before he could call for her again, he lost consciousness and floated deeper into the rainbow portal on his way to Zentobia.

Within a matter of seconds, the colorful arch disappeared, and a pile of dirt and rocks covered the ground. Penny sobbed uncontrollably for minutes and then wiped her wet cheeks.

"He will bring back the kids. They have to make it home," she muttered and walked away.

CHAPTER NINETEEN

Griffen woke in Zentobia, disoriented from the ride he'd just endured. Chatter from a distance kept his trained ears alert. He inched his wobbly body up and tried to shake the feeling that he was dreaming.

"We made it!" Mr. Drop yelled from a few feet away. He stood and trotted over to Griffen. "You okay? Welcome to Zentobia."

Where is Penny? He tripped over his unsteady feet and scanned the area, looking for her.

As he got his bearings, he glimpsed someone flying above his head. "What the heck am I seeing up there?" He pointed to the people flying in the sky.

"It must be morning rush hour. They're going to work. We have a lot of beautiful lakes and rivers in the south side of the world, so it's much faster to fly over them. Before I... err...left here, I dispensed the flying shoes. I would love to get my job back. And I have to see my family. After we find the kids."

"I don't see Penny anywhere." He turned full-circle. "Do you think she could have landed somewhere else?"

Mr. Drop shook his head. "She most likely didn't have enough time to go through. It's probably for the best that she stays in Hailsville in case the kids make it back while we're still here. Ahh...it seems like only yesterday when I was a boy. I would run through some of these same fields. It sure is good to be home!"

"Wonderful memories." *That we don't have time for.* "Let's go. Where to first?" Griffen spotted his backpack a few feet away and grabbed it.

"Our best bet is to head toward Minka's palace. She's the leader of the south and would know if two kids from another world were here. Follow me. It's not far."

As they headed to the palace, Griffen took photographs with his eyes of everything in sight. Small homes appeared along the way with bold hues that popped against a picturesque backdrop of lush green grass and thick trees that ran up to jagged mountains at every corner in the distance. Several waterfalls trickled down the mountains, but he couldn't see where the water ended. "This place looks like something straight out of a fairy tale."

The palace sparkled in the distance. Covered in glittering gold and flecks of silver, the building rose several floors and spanned across many acres. Sturdy glass windows glistened behind iron security bars that fronted many of them. High above the palace, a shiny gold star illuminated the sky.

"Is that the star you told me about?" Griffen asked.

"Yes. It's the only gold one in this world and gives us light, kind of like your sun. The others are all black and visible only in the north. It's much darker there."

"What happened to them?"

"It's more like *who* happened to them. Cyrus, the ruler of northern Zentobia, turned them black. If the last gold star turns black, he could use dark magic again. If that happens, the whole world would be in danger."

"That doesn't sound good. Hope we don't run into this Cyrus guy."

Mr. Drop put a gentle hand on Griffen's shoulder and motioned to follow him toward the palace. "The palace is the oldest building in Zentobia. It's invitation-only for a visit."

Griffen stopped walking. "So, what does that mean? They won't let us in?"

"I'm sure once we explain who we are and why we are here, they'll let us enter and see Minka."

They walked up to the gate, where a dozen armed men stood.

Griffen sized up the guards. Dark brown, well-fitted uniforms made them all look like they meant business. Sleek weapons resembling guns hung from thin belts that fit snugly around their waists. "What's the plan here?" He checked behind him to make sure he felt his backpack.

"Let me do all the talking," Mr. Drop said.

They approached the guards.

"Hello, I'm Mr. Drop...I mean, Mr. Walric, and this is Griffen. We are here to see Minka."

Griffen looked at him in surprise. It had never crossed his mind that Drop wasn't his real name.

"One moment," a guard said. Half of them walked into the palace.

"Walric?" Griffen whispered.

"Yes. When I arrived in Hailsville, I couldn't remember my name. I was so disoriented. Drop came to mind, so I ran with it. It wasn't until we arrived back here that I remembered it."

The guards returned and waved them through the entrance.

"You did it, *Walric*. Nice job."

A few minutes passed on the walk from the gate to the palace. A path set between rows of colorful stones led to the oversized, shiny gold door. They followed the guards inside, and the smell of fresh flowers reminiscent of the ones he'd given Penny on their last anniversary greeted him. A spiral staircase, floating from side to side like ocean waves, dangled directly in front of them, while a library with books shifting from shelf to shelf sat to their left. Straight ahead, a long corridor with hovering doors on both sides encompassed an enormous part of the main floor. Griffen got dizzy as his head darted from the staircase to the library to the doors and back to the staircase.

A small bird and chunky dog waddled over.

"Minka will see you now," Talia said. "Follow us."

Griffen's jaw dropped. "What the heck was that? Did that bird just *talk*?"

"Yep, she sure did," Chester said. "All us animals can talk. Get used to it."

Griffen shook his head. First flying people, and now talking animals. McCall would never believe this, nor would anyone.

Talia and Chester led them down the long corridor and into a spacious room. Minka's simple brown dress blended into the dark wooden desk she sat behind. The room had a separate area with a blue couch, two cushioned chairs, and a smooth, dark table. Talia jumped up and sat on Minka's desk, and Chester plopped down on the shaggy rug in front of the couch. Within seconds, the dog's snoring filled the room.

Minka leaped to her feet. "Mr. Walric! We've been very

worried. I speak to your family all the time. Where have you been? Are you okay?" Her eyes glistened as she spoke.

Griffen studied her carefully. His profession trained him to know if someone tried to deceive him. He examined her body movements and facial expressions as Mr. Walric explained his story.

"Thank you for keeping in touch with my family. I've been trying to get home for a while now. It's a long story, and we have little time, because we're looking for two children." He retold the events that had occurred in Hailsville. "It wasn't until Maggie and Peter helped me find the location of the rainbow's end that I figured out how to get home. I'm afraid they went through the rainbow portal on their own first and might have ended up here. Have you seen them?"

She looked away. "That sounds like a very troublesome ordeal. I'm so sorry. But you are home now, and your family will be so happy. We should get word to them immediately." She turned to Griffen. "And who is this?"

"Name's Griffen. My kids are somewhere in this world, and I'm here to get them back. I would appreciate any help you could provide."

She clasped her hands together in front of her. "Yes, your kids were here. I did everything I could to make sure they were safe, but we believe they ran off after we gave them dinner."

"Ran off? Well, at least they had dinner first. What do you mean, *ran off*? Where do you think they ran off to?"

She walked over to Chester and nudged his pudgy, wrinkled face. The dog snored even louder. She jabbed him again. "Chester! Wake up! I need you to tell our guests about Maggie and Peter."

The dog rolled on his back and threw his legs in the air

to stretch.

"Great, we are relying on a lazy mutt that eats and sleeps all day to help find my kids," Griffen muttered.

Chester snorted through his pushed-in nose and rolled back over, facing Griffen. "I heard that. As for your kids, they tricked me into finishing their dinner so they could sneak out. Maggie had to use the restroom, and they both went to find it down the hall. But instead of coming back, they disappeared."

"Did anyone try to find them?"

"Yes, I sent Talia, Chester, and some of my guards to follow their trail, but we lost them when they headed too far north," Minka said.

"North?" Griffen's blood pressure rose. He turned to Mr. Walric. "But isn't that the part of the world you told me to stay far away from?"

Mr. Walric nodded. "I assume Cyrus still rules the northern part of the world?"

"That's correct. If they traveled to the north side, Cyrus will probably find them, and there's nothing we can do to help them."

Griffen's breath blew flames as hot as fire coming out of a dragon's mouth. His heart pounded louder than a drum, but he tried to contain his anger to secure Minka's help. He walked over to her, clutching his hands. "I get that a psycho rules the north side of the world, and everyone over there is evil, but I will get my kids back. I would love some help, but if you can't help me, then at least show me the way to get to this Cyrus guy so I can talk some sense into him."

She walked to the window. Lights were visible coming from inside the homes on the outskirts of town.

"There is no reasoning with Cyrus. He will hold the kids ransom for some ridiculous demand. Or, he would make you and the kids his slaves." She turned to Griffen. "But there might be a way we can help each other. Cyrus is trying to destroy this side of the world so he can become the sole ruler. He is controlling our weather and making it rain more than it should, which is killing our land. We accidentally discovered that the extra rain opens the rainbow portal and the soil from your world brings new life to our land." She went to her desk and pulled out a glass jar filled with soil. Griffen eyed it curiously. "Cyrus doesn't know this, and if we can continue to stockpile the soil, we can keep him at bay. Your police have noticed our people removing the soil. If you can keep your police away from us, I will help you get your kids back."

Her story didn't come as too much of a surprise to Griffen, since they'd already put many of the pieces together about Zentobia. Removing the soil seemed harmless enough, though being involved in a dispute with another world didn't sound that good. He could worry about that later, he thought. Agreeing with her to get his kids back seemed the way to go.

"I'll do it." He held out his hand for her to shake, but she ignored the gesture. "One more thing. Has anyone else from Hailsville shown up here? We've had some people go missing. I think they might have fallen into the portal by accident."

"We haven't seen anyone else in the south side of the world, but that doesn't mean they didn't end up in the north. If they did, Cyrus most likely has them."

"I would sure like to find that out. What do we do now?"

"First, Mr. Walric, you go home to your family and enjoy the reunion," she said. "Griffen, we have some planning to do. Getting into the north side of the world is not easy, but

I have some tricks. There's an underground tunnel system that my father built that runs from the north to the south. If we follow the right route, it will lead us straight to Cyrus' palace. I'm sure that's where he's holding the kids."

"Okay, great, let's go." Griffen walked to the door.

"Not so fast. Finding the entrance to the tunnels will take time. When my father built them, he cast a shifting spell that made the entrance disappear and move to a new spot every couple of days. We'll have to send out the squirrels to find the entrance. Once they find it, we can go."

Griffen clenched his fists and put them on his hips. "Okay, then deploy the squirrels. Send out the cats, the birds, the monkeys, and the rabbits if you have to. Send out every animal on this side of the world to find that entrance. Wait...did you say spell? Like a magic spell?"

"Yes, a magic spell." She walked over to the phone and lifted the receiver.

He addressed Mr. Walric. "You didn't mention there's magic here. Is this for real?"

"When Minka's father ruled Zentobia, magic had a large role in this world. But it was banished after he had a deadly falling-out with Cyrus's father. Minka is the only one permitted to practice, and only if there is a threat."

"What happ—?"

The bang from the phone receiver demanded their attention.

"It's done," Minka said. "The squirrels are heading out now to find the tunnel entrance. If all goes well, we should be on our way to the north by nightfall. Once you set foot in the tunnels, you move twice as fast as you would above ground without ever realizing it."

"More magic?" Griffen asked.

Minka smiled. "Yes."

Griffen put a hand on Mr. Walric's shoulder. "I guess this is where we part ways. Thanks for getting me here."

"I'm sorry your kids ended up in this situation. I would like to come with you to help get them back."

"Thanks, but it's unnecessary. You've been away from your family for a long time. Go be with them. I think we're covered here."

Mr. Walric's breathing became shallow, and he dragged his feet toward the door.

Two guards burst into the room, almost knocking Mr. Walric over. Peter stood behind them.

Griffen bolted to him. "Peter! I thought you and Maggie ran away from here?" Griffen squeezed Peter in his arms.

Peter tried to catch his breath. "We did, but...Dad, we have to save Maggie. A guy in a cape with a bunch of owls kidnapped her!"

Minka and Mr. Walric looked at each other.

"Cyrus!" Minka said.

Peter spotted Mr. Walric over his dad's shoulder. "Oh, hey, Mr. Drop. You got my dad here. Thank you!"

Mr. Walric nodded. "You're welcome."

"How did you get away and not Maggie?" his dad asked.

"It's a long story, but I ran ahead and kinda escaped getting captured so I could come back here to get help."

"That was very brave of you to decide to leave your sister behind and get help. Now, we are going to get her." He faced Minka. "So, what's the plan when we get to Cyrus' palace? How many men will we storm in there with? Do you have the layout of the place so I know where we are going?"

"Oh no. We will not storm in with our men. I don't believe in using force. We'll have a discussion, and he will return the kids."

Griffen threw up his hands. "Forgive me, but didn't you

tell me that this man is nuts and would enslave me and the kids? How do you expect to have a civilized discussion with a guy like this?"

"Because we will sneak in and, shall I say, borrow his children first. We will trade his kids for Maggie."

He put his hands on his hips and smiled. "That will work."

CHAPTER TWENTY

Maggie didn't speak much during the stressful journey to Cyrus' palace, and the owls didn't talk to her either. The whole way there, strange noises rang in her ears, and she prayed the owls wouldn't stop to eat her. Upon arrival at the palace, she wanted to take out her journal but decided against it in case the mean old owl snatched it away. She would have to write the description of the palace later, especially the bizarre white mannequins wearing different-colored capes. *What is it with this guy and capes?* Drab black walls stood in every direction, and her sneakers skidded over white marble flooring covered with specks of dirt. Dusty photographs of Cyrus wearing different-colored capes hung on the walls. She even spotted a black widow crawling up one photo. *Does anyone ever clean this place?*

The owls took her down a set of stairs and through a hallway. As they made their way down the corridor, people inside locked rooms banged on the walls. Others were sleeping, and some stared with sorrow-filled eyes. Their haggard clothing reminded her of the people she used to feed with her family when they went to the homeless shelter on weekends. *What is this place?*

They reached an empty room, and the owls shoved her inside.

She sat on the floor, staring at the plain walls. The only sound came from the chatter of her teeth. Her chilled body shivered. *How am I going to get out of here? I don't think my bathroom trick will work on these owls.* She stood and shuffled her feet as she paced the small room.

The door swung open, and Screech entered with food and a drink. "Here, eat this." The grumpy owl slammed the door on his way out.

"Wait!" she screamed. "Let me out of here!" A strong whiff of the food prompted her to peer down at it. It smelled like leftover egg salad that had been in the refrigerator for several days too long. She took a seat next to it, wondering if it tasted as bad as it smelled. She reached for the spoon but pulled her hand back.

Green soup with brown bits floating in it bubbled in the bowl. *This looks nothing like the stuff Minka gave me and Peter. And it doesn't smell like split pea with ham. It could be poison, or worse, dead rabbit soup or something.*

The door opened again, and she slid back as far as she could into the icy wall. The smell of rotten egg salad intensified.

"Ah, my new friend, how are you enjoying your food?" asked Cyrus, his oversized cape dragging along the floor behind him. "Don't worry, it's not poisoned, if that's what you're thinking. I'm not a monster. It's time we get to know each other. I want to learn everything about where you came from and how you got here. Start talking."

Maggie averted her eyes from Cyrus when a cheekbone pierced through his pale skin. *If I tell the truth, will Cyrus want to go to Hailsville? Will he kill me once I reveal all the secrets? I have to stall.*

"Look, Mr. Cyrus, I would really love to see your palace and get to know this side of the world better." She hoped he would be receptive to compliments, but she could tell by his gaze of steel that he didn't like the idea.

Cyrus twirled the sides of his cape, commanding her attention. "My power reigns supreme in the north, and the south is long overdue for an awakening." He ran his crooked fingers up the side of the wall like they were weaving a spiderweb.

"How many people do you rule over?"

He clenched his hands on his hips. "That depends on how you look at things. Technically, there are several thousand people who live in the north. And, soon, the thousands of people who live in the south will join us. And if you include the hundreds of animals scattered all over, that brings the total even higher."

"It seems like you're a super smart ruler." She stood and faced him, her body trembling. *Stay calm. Keep stalling.* "Maybe Screech can show me around?"

He walked to Maggie and pointed his finger at her nose. She could smell the stench of something rotten on his finger and gagged. "We don't have time for a tour or any small talk. I received word that two more visitors have arrived in Zentobia, and perhaps they're here to find you? If they are, I will stop them immediately unless you tell me everything about how you got here."

Maggie's heart skipped a beat. It had to be Mr. Drop and their dad, or her dad and mom. It didn't matter as long as someone came to save her and find Peter. Telling Cyrus the truth might be the only way to stall until someone rescued her.

"Okay...I will tell you." She divulged a short, edited version of how she'd arrived in Zentobia. She left out the part about her dad being a detective and meeting Minka.

"Fascinating!" Drool escaped the side of his mouth. "When the other visitors told me they came from another world, I didn't believe them and ordered them to work for me. But if you are telling me the same thing, it must be true. If I have a way to bring more people to the north side of this world, I could create the largest following anyone has ever seen!" He threw his cape over his boney shoulders, swiping the sides of his eccentric face as it fell back.

"The people in the other rooms...are they part of your *following*?"

"Ah yes, those prison—I mean, guests. They have all committed crimes. My corrections squad caught them in the act and brought them here. They are serving out their sentence with an *opportunity* to work in my laborat—I mean, factory."

Keep him talking. "What kind of factory?"

"It's an important facility where I'm working on fine-tuning a special device to bring back black mag—" His eyes grew wider as he spoke. "Something that will help me change the world."

"How will it change the world?"

Screech entered the room and waved Cyrus over. The owl whispered something in his ear.

A crooked smile formed on Cyrus' face, and he moved to the door to leave.

"Wait...Now that I told you everything, will you let me go?" Maggie asked.

"Silly child." Cyrus walked over and patted her head. "How can I let you go when you haven't even shown me this

89

rainbow portal yet? I must see it for myself. We'll leave in the morning."

He left the room as abruptly as he'd entered it.

Maggie's eyes welled with tears. Dread filled her veins at spending the night in the cold, empty room. She twisted the doorknob, but it didn't turn. "Help! Let me out of here!"

"There's no way out," a voice said.

Where is that voice coming from? A room next door? "Hello? Who are you? Where are you?"

"I'm in the room next to you. My name is Jax."

"I'm Maggie. How long have you been down here?"

Jax did not reply.

Maggie pressed her ear against the door. "Hello?"

"I lost track of time. Maybe a year."

Her voice cracked. "A year?" She pulled her ear away from the door and looked around the room again for anything that might help her escape. But only a bed and a chair occupied the small space. "I'm going to help get everyone out of here. My family is coming for me."

"That's what I thought too. But I'm still here."

She forced back the tears and sat on the chair. *I'm going to get us out of here somehow. There has to be a way.*

CHAPTER TWENTY-ONE

Three dozen squeaking squirrels scurried their little feet all over the south side of the world, looking for the entrance to the secret tunnels. They were on a tight timeframe to cross through them at night.

In Minka's office, Peter sat on the couch watching his dad pace the floor while they waited for word on when they would leave. He already got a first-hand look at his dad's skills as a detective. Moments ago, Larz, the head guard, gave his dad a lesson on how to use their fancy guns that shot sleeping darts. Then his dad brought him in on the action to help study the floor plan of Cyrus's palace. *I can get used to this detective stuff.*

The door jarred open, and Minka, dressed in all black, entered with her guards.

"The squirrels found the entrance. It's time to go. Once we get there, we'll stick to the plan. Get Cyrus' kids and make the trade to get Maggie back."

"How can you be sure Cyrus will let us go after we return his kids?" Griffen asked.

"Leave that to me. It will be an ultimatum he won't be able to refuse."

They followed Minka and the guards out of the palace. A small group of squirrels waited outside the front door.

"This way," said one of the tiny squirrels. The squirrels rushed through the palace grounds and around several winding pathways.

Everyone followed close behind.

The group approached what looked like an ordinary field of grass. The squirrels' little arms and legs cut through the grass faster than a bullet train racing down the tracks.

"Whoa...look at them go," Peter said.

An old wooden door covered in cracks appeared, and one of Minka's guards pulled back on the rusty lever to open it. A rickety staircase with gaping holes in the stairs led straight down into complete darkness.

Peter squinted as he looked into the black hole. *No way am I going down there.*

"Take it easy on the stairs. They haven't been used in a long time," Minka said.

"Like thousands of years?" Peter asked, staring at the pieces missing from the staircase. "Are you sure this is a good idea?"

"It will be fine. They look worse than they are," Minka said. She went down the stairs, placing one foot gently on each one at a time. "Follow me."

I don't know about this. Peter put his right foot on the stair, and it sank as he added more weight. "I think it's going to break." He held his breath and carefully crept down the rest of the stairs. *Made it. Phew!*

When they all reached the dimly-lit bottom, Minka said, "Let's go, and stay close. It's been a while since I've been through here. I don't know what might have changed."

"What do you mean, what might have changed? What could change in a tunnel?" Griffen asked. "Oh, I almost forgot, the tunnel entrance changes every couple of days."

"The configuration and direction of the pathways change frequently. My father used magic to put in safeguards. I promised him I would only come down here in a true emergency. I think this qualifies."

Griffen put his hands on his hips and shook his head.

"Don't worry. As a kid, I spent a lot of time navigating down here. I have a good idea of where to go."

The group headed deep into the winding tunnels. The sound of their footsteps echoed along the way.

A few minutes passed, and Peter expected a creepy spider or gigantic rat to pop out at him. Fortunately, the subtle glow of light from the suspended lamps provided a clear path. The weathered walls looked like manmade stone, marked with symbols and three-dimensional shapes.

Minka stopped every so often to study the floating animal statues they passed. "The whisking arms and legs of these little creatures signal directional clues."

Peter walked over to one statue that looked like a bear. He ran his arm above and below it to inspect for wires or anything that might help keep it afloat. "How are these things staying up? They look so heavy." He placed his hand on it.

Minka ran to him. "Peter, don't touch that!"

Before anyone could react, the floor crumbled, and they all dropped a level below.

Piles of rocks and rubble surrounded everyone. Groans echoed off the walls.

"Peter!" Griffen shuffled away the debris that covered his body. "Are you okay?"

"Yeah. I think so." Peter pushed aside the stones and sat up. "I'm sorry. This is all my fault."

Griffen made his way to Peter and helped him up. "It's okay. You had no idea. At least we fell with the floor and it didn't fall on top of us. Let's find Minka." He plowed through the scattered wreckage on the floor. "Minka? Where are you?"

She stood off to the side, looking at the space above them. "I'm over here. I think I know how to get us out of here."

Peter ran to her. "I'm so sorry."

She placed a hand on his shoulder. "I know. I should have warned everyone not to touch anything. Especially the floating animals."

"Another one of your father's safeguards?" Griffen asked.

"I'm afraid so. Where are Larz and the guards?" She searched for them. "Larz? Larz?"

Larz's head peered through a mound of stones that covered his body. "Yeah."

The group rushed over and scooped away the rubble. The other guards joined them to help.

"Can you move?" Griffen asked. He extended a hand to pull Larz up.

"Yes. I'm okay." Larz regained his balance and dusted himself off.

Griffen looked at Minka and pointed to the floor above. "Well then, how are we going to get back up there?"

"Does anyone have a rope?" Minka asked. "If we can get the rope around the bear statue that caused this, it will anchor us up."

Griffen shuffled through his backpack. "I've got one right here."

"Great. You think you can lasso it around the bear?"

Peter laughed. His dad didn't have the best aim. Especially at basketball. *Maybe this will be different. I hope.*

"Only one way to find out." Griffen tied a knot in the rope and left a hoop large enough to circle the bear. He threw it up several times with no luck.

"Can I try?" Peter asked.

Griffen handed Peter the rope, and he landed it around the bear on his second try. "Nice job. Why don't you climb up there first and see if there's enough flooring left to hold all of us so we can get out of here."

Peter looked up, the floating statues glaring back down at him. "Uh...I...don't know...What if those statues come to life or something?"

"That won't happen unless you touch them," Minka said.

I can do this. Just don't touch anything. He nodded and placed his hands on the rope. His dad helped push him up. The floor above wasn't too high, making it an easy climb. When he got to the top, he inspected the area. "Uh, guys...We've got a problem."

"What is it?" his dad asked.

"A piece of the floor is missing where we need to cross. It's too big of a hole to jump to the other side."

"How long is the gap in the floor?" His dad searched for anything sturdy they could use as a bridge to walk across.

"Guessing it's about ten feet."

"Everything is in pieces down here." He approached Minka. "Is there another way out?"

Minka lowered her head. "There is *something* I can do."

Larz put a hand on Minka's shoulder. "Are you sure?"

"Yes. It's the fastest way out of this situation."

Griffen threw up his hands. "Anyone like to tell me what you're talking about?"

"I will cast a spell to create a bridge so we can get across the gap. It's just—"

Larz interrupted. "This will be the first time she's used magic in a *very* long time." He turned to Minka. "It's okay. You have no choice."

Minka called up to Peter. "Peter, move back from the hole as far as you can."

"Okay."

She recited a spell. "The floor above from side to side, build a bridge to let us glide."

Within seconds, a bridge materialized, closing the gap in the floor.

Peter's eyes grew as wide as Mr. Walric's mustache. "Whoa! You guys will *not* believe this." He bounced a foot on the bridge, and it didn't crumble. "A walkway just appeared out of nowhere."

"Just stay put, Peter. We're on our way up." Griffen handed Minka the rope. "After you."

The group made their way to the top. They hurried across the bridge and stopped on the other side.

"Everyone okay?" Griffen asked.

"Yeah, but how did that bridge get there?" Peter asked.

"Just a little Zentobian magic," Minka said.

"We can talk more about that later, Peter," his dad said. "Good job getting up here to let us know about the floor. But keep your hands to yourself the rest of the way." He turned to Minka. "Where else do these tunnels lead?"

"I'm not sure," she said. "There's a specific route I have to follow to get to the north side based upon the signals of the statues. If we deviate from that route, we'll end up somewhere else."

"Let's not find that out today." He walked side-by-side

with her, small pebbles making crackling noises under his feet.

After what seemed like hours, she stopped. "We're here." She pulled out a floor plan from a pouch around her waist. "What is this, Larz? This is the floor plan of *my* palace."

Larz stepped over to look. He wiped his wet brows, removing the beads of sweat.

"Sorry. That's the wrong one." He pulled a folded floor plan out of his pocket and handed it haphazardly to her. "Here are the schematics of Cyrus's palace."

She took the paper and studied it. "According to these plans, we should be right near the side entrance of the palace where Cyrus only stations one guard. We'll take cover here, at this adjacent building. As soon as the guard goes on his break, that's our chance to enter the palace. The guards inside should all be asleep this time of night. The side entrance connects to a hallway that leads straight to Cyrus' kids' room. We'll grab the kids and bring them back to the tunnel. Put these blindfolds on the kids before you bring them to the tunnel so they can't disclose the entrance to their father." She handed Larz two blindfolds. "We'll remain here until morning, when Cyrus realizes they're gone. Then, as we planned, we'll broker the deal to exchange his kids for Maggie."

"You sound like you have brokered a lot of these deals before," Griffen said.

"No, but I learned quite a bit from my father. This will be my first deal, and it's long overdue. Everyone ready?"

They all nodded.

Minka walked up a wobbly staircase to exit the tunnel.

Peter paused at the bottom of the stairs. *Oh, great,*

another staircase. Here goes nothing. He walked up, and the rest of the crew followed.

At the top, Minka pushed the door open and climbed out, with Peter close behind.

Just as she indicated, the side entrance of the palace came into view, and only one guard paced back and forth in front of the door. They took cover behind a compact building next to the palace, most likely the maids' quarters, according to the floor plan.

"Look, the guard is heading out," Larz said. "Let's move. Minka, get back inside the tunnel with Peter and wait there. We'll get the kids and bring them to you." Larz, Griffen, and two other guards headed over to the side entrance of the palace to execute the plan.

CHAPTER TWENTY-TWO

In her bedroom in Cyrus' palace, Santori's droopy eyes stared at the stale white ceiling. She didn't even bother to change out of her mismatched clothes and into pajamas. Sleepless nights were common for her, something she hoped to outgrow by her upcoming fourteenth birthday.

As the daughter of the most feared man in Zentobia, Santori struggled to find a balance between power and happiness as she desperately tried to make her father proud. While Cyrus groomed her sixteen-year-old brother Krado to rule alongside him, he trained Santori to befriend all the female young adults on the north side of the world to secure their loyalty. It wasn't that hard, since most of the teenage girls wanted to know everything about her, right down to her skin care and makeup routines.

As she did every night, she reached underneath her pillow and took out a small videograph of a woman who looked to be in her early twenties. The woman's long, flowing brown hair and blue eyes complimented her silky, ivory skin.

"Are you looking at that old videograph again?" Krado

jumped his long-limbed, slender body out of bed and turned the light on. "You know, the quality is far more advanced now. That one has got to be at least five years old."

"Ugh. I know that. How do you even know about this videograph? What are you doing awake?"

"I see you looking at it every night." He brushed the overgrown, thick black hair away from his pale face. "Who is it?"

"I can't wait to get back into my room when these renovations are over. You're always in my business. And this videograph is none of your concern."

In the blink of an eye, Krado leaped over and snatched the box out of Santori's loose grip. He pressed play and looked at the short video with curious eyes. She jumped out of bed and tried to pull the cube out of Krado's boney hands but had no luck.

"Who the heck is this?" He ran around the room waving the videograph in the air.

"Give it back now!" She chased him wildly. Her fair skin turned beet red.

"Not until you tell me who this woman is and why you obsess over her." He tripped on his long, checkered pajama pants and landed sideways on the floor.

"Ha! That's what you get!" She snickered with the same sneer she liked to flaunt at Krado when she beat him at their favorite trivia game, Tondu. Pleased with her win, she stopped chasing him, wrapped her messy brown hair into a bun on top of her head, and sat down on her bed. "It's our mother, if you must know. I *borrowed* that videograph from Dad a long time ago. He showed it to me once when he told me a story about her. After he put it back inside his desk, I took it. I don't even think he knows it's missing. I just wonder what it would be like if she was still alive and with us today."

"How come Dad never showed this to me? He shows me everything."

"Did you ever even ask to see any videographs of our mother? Seems like all you care about is walking in our father's footsteps. Don't you remember the stories he used to tell us when we were little?" She leaned against the wall and pushed the covers aside.

She cherished the stories her father told about her mother. He would sit her and Krado down after dinner and tell them how brave and smart she was and how she loved them both very much. He didn't speak of her anymore, and he offered no information about the accident he said caused her death. Santori always wondered what had happened and hoped one day she would find out the truth. Until then, she had the videograph to keep her mother's memory alive.

"Yeah, I remember. But what good does it do me now?"

"You are so cold and heartless." A scuffling noise coming from the hallway caught her attention. She leaped off the bed and plucked the videograph out of Krado's hands. "Sounds like the guards are awake."

Before she could investigate the noise, the bedroom door swung open. Larz and Griffen sprang inside.

"Any noise you make could hurt your father," Griffen said. "They have him at gunpoint in his office. Follow us quietly so we can get you out of here before they come for you too."

Santori stuffed the videograph of her mother into her pocket and quickly found a pair of shoes. She moved to the door.

Krado resisted. "Who the heck are you? What are you doing in my palace? We are not going anywhere with you."

"We have little time. Some unwelcome visitors from the south are here. They are being dealt with." Griffen used some of his best acting skills he'd learned from playing make-believe with Maggie. "We are part of a secret security detail your father put together just for you. We have to go now. Follow us."

Santori knew Krado wouldn't need any other explanation after hearing he had his own security detail.

He nodded, grabbed his shoes, and walked to the door.

The four of them ran down the hall and out the side door of the palace, where they encountered Minka's other two guards.

Griffen stopped everyone before heading to the tunnel entrance. "Aren't you forgetting something, Larz?"

"I don't think so. What?"

He pointed to the blindfolds in Larz's pocket.

"Oh yeah. Almost forgot about those." He took the eye coverings out and handed one to Griffen. "We have to put these on you for your own safety, because we're going to a secure location."

"If it's such a secure location and you are *my* security detail, then whether I need these should be my decision," Krado fired back.

Larz took hold of his arm, pulling him forward. "There's no time to debate this." He fastened the blindfold around Krado's crossed eyes.

Krado swatted at Larz's arms. "You don't have to make it that tight."

They guided the kids back to the tunnel entrance. Larz brushed aside the shrubs covering the door and took off the kid's blindfolds.

"Whoa...what is this and what's down there?" Krado

asked. "I'm not going into any dungeon. I'll be just fine up here where I can see everything."

"It's not a dungeon. Follow me and we'll explain," Larz said.

They filed down the stairs. Griffen stood by Peter. Larz, along with the two guards, retreated next to the other security men who stood in a tight line in front of Minka. Slowly, they parted, and Minka stepped between them, facing Krado and Santori.

"I'm sorry you're here under these circumstances," Minka said. "Have some water. We'll be here for a while." She handed the water to Krado and Santori.

Santori couldn't take her eyes off Minka. She stared at the gentle blue eyes that gazed back at her effortlessly. The woman's fair-skinned face beamed through waves of long brown hair. A lump formed in her throat, and she reached for the videograph.

"My father will not be happy that his new, I mean *my* security detail, isn't telling me what's happening in the palace. And who the heck are you?" Krado asked Minka as he took a swig of water.

"Krado...is that any way to talk to our...mother?" Santori asked.

The water caught in Krado's throat and gushed out of his mouth. "What are you talking about? Our mother is dead."

Santori stared at the videograph cube, then back at Minka, and shoved it in Krado's face. "Look at her, and look at the woman in this video. They're identical." She took the box and walked closer to Minka. She held it up for Minka to see. "Is it true? Is this you?"

Griffen's jaw dropped as he got a glimpse of the woman in the small electronic device.

"Yes, Santori. I'm your mother." Tears spilled down Minka's face. "I have so much to tell you."

"But our father—he told us you were dead?" Santori held back tears. She didn't know whether to be angry or happy. "He said there was an accident. Didn't you want to be with us?"

"Obviously not, if she hasn't shown her face until now," Krado said. He turned to Minka. "So we have a videograph that looks like you. That's not proof. Why are we here anyway? When is our father going to get here? He can clear this all up."

"Unfortunately, Cyrus is the one that put us in this position. We are separated because of his quest for power. And I have waited all these years to tell you what happened. I married Cyrus before Zentobia divided into the north and south, when we still practiced magic. Back then, the world was separated into quadrants. My father, Mortis, your grandfather, ruled over each quadrant. When it became too much for him, he gave Cyrus the authority to rule one quadrant. That's when he got his first taste of power and dark magic, and it drove him to want more. After I became pregnant and had Krado, your father promised he would take a step back and spend more time with us. But that never happened. His quest for power and magic grew stronger." She walked to Santori. "When I became pregnant with you, Cyrus used dark magic and turned five of Zentobia's six gold stars black. But when my father had a dispute with your dad's father, who ultimately met his demise, he stripped Cyrus of his magical abilities, and it spared the last gold star. If that star turns black, Cyrus will use dark magic again, and that would be very dangerous for our world."

Krado turned to Santori. "Are you believing any of this?"

"I don't know what to believe."

Minka put a hand on Santori's shoulder. "After you were born, Cyrus secretly tried to turn everyone against my father. When the north side died, he saw that as his opportunity to step in and take it over."

A chuckle escaped from Krado's mouth. "Now that sounds like Dad's kind of plan."

"Shut up!" Santori said.

"Cyrus gave me an ultimatum. Unless we all joined him in the north, he would employ his corrections team to enslave everyone in the south that didn't become one of his followers. Or, I could give you and Krado up for good and remain in the south on my own with your grandfather and our people. I knew he wanted to groom the two of you to rule by his side, and I had a tough decision to make. I could not let him enslave all those people, and let me assure you, he would have. I knew he would not harm you, because he was your father. So, I did what I thought was best. It was the hardest thing I ever had to do in my life. But now, I know I made a mistake not coming for you sooner."

"Why did it take you so long? Why now?" Santori asked.

"There are several reasons. Your father found a way to control the weather in the south to make it rain." Minka looked at Griffen. "Recently, I met a man who is here to save his kids. He reminded me that there is nothing more important than having his children by his side and what he would risk to achieve that."

"Is that guy you?" Krado asked Griffen.

"Yeah, that *guy* is me," Griffen said. "One of my kids is being held captive by your father. I'm here to get her back."

"I will give your father an ultimatum," Minka said. "If he returns Griffen's daughter, then I will return you both to him."

"But what if I don't want to go?" Santori asked. "I mean,

I just met you. It's not fair." She inched closer to Minka's side.

"What about any of this is fair?" Krado said. "They took us from our home in the middle of the night, disrupting our sleep. Don't be so quick to believe this is even our mother."

Santori knew Minka was her mother. The videograph she'd kept hidden under her pillow for so long came to life. The promise of a relationship with her mom stood right in front of her.

"When can we get out of this horrible place?" Krado asked.

"Larz will go to the palace in the morning to speak to your father," Minka said. "Then it will be up to him when you get out of here. Have a seat and get comfortable. We'll be here for a while."

The grunt that came out of Krado's mouth echoed throughout the tunnel. He slumped into a corner of the room, shuffling away the dust and dirt on the floor with his feet.

Minka took Santori aside and spent the hours ahead talking to her daughter.

CHAPTER TWENTY-THREE

A bright sun peered through small cracks in the tunnel entrance as the long night evolved into morning. Larz made his way over to the palace. Griffen paced back and forth, eager to make the exchange with Cyrus.

Krado's body, curled up under the stairs, melted into the wall. His snores echoed throughout the tunnel. *Let him sleep,* Santori thought. *He would just interfere with the time I spend with my mother.* The more she talked with Minka, the more she thought about what it would be like to go to the south side of the world to start a new life. She knew her father would never stand for it, but maybe another way could work instead.

The tunnel door creaked open.

Krado's head sprang up. "Where am I? What's happening?" A room full of people stared back at him.

Santori laughed, exchanging a discreet glance with Minka.

Larz ran down the stairs and tripped over Krado's feet, stumbling into Griffen.

Griffen flew backward and slammed into the wall. He

wobbled and gained his footing. "I know we're all tired from a long night, but let's get it together, people. Larz, did anyone see you enter the tunnel? What did Cyrus say?"

"I don't think anyone followed me. I had a not-so-pleasant chat with Cyrus. But he's willing to make the exchange. If we bring Santori and Krado to the side entrance of the palace in thirty minutes, he'll have Maggie there."

Griffen sighed. "What guarantee do we have that if we bring his kids to the palace, he'll give us Maggie? If this guy is as devious as you all say he is, how do we know his guards won't storm us, grab his kids, and take us prisoner?"

"That's why I should stay behind as leverage," Santori blurted. "Let me remain down here while you make the exchange with Krado. Once you have your daughter back, tell my father I will come up."

"I think that could work," Griffen said. "Minka, you okay with it? It might be our only way to ensure we get Maggie back."

Minka put an arm around Santori, bringing her in close. "Are you sure?"

"I am. I want to do this."

"Okay, then. Larz, you take Griffen and two guards and head over to the palace with Krado. Make the exchange, and when you return safely, we'll send Santori over," Minka said.

Griffen nudged Krado to stand, and he begrudgingly rose to his feet.

The group walked up the stairs and out the tunnel entrance.

Larz pulled out the blindfold to put on Krado. Before he could, Krado looked back at his sister and shook his head.

Santori gave him a sly wink. Her plan to stay behind with Minka had worked like a charm.

Peter walked over to Santori. "What are you up to?"

"What do you mean? I was the one taken from my home. I'm not up to anything."

"If you mess up the plan to get my sister back, then…"

Santori raised her brows. "Then what? I think out of everyone here, you have the least to say about what happens."

"We'll see about that." Peter stormed off. He took a seat in the corner and waited.

CHAPTER TWENTY-FOUR

Maggie barely slept all night in the dark room inside Cyrus' palace. After she finally dozed off, two guards stormed in and woke her up.

"Get up!" yelled a guard. "Hurry, we have to move. Now!"

Dazed, she inched her sleepy body up and followed the guards out the door.

Cyrus glared at her as she approached. His threadlike fingers fiddled to clasp the hook together on his red cape. "You have uninvited visitors. This put a kink in my plan to go to the rainbow this morning, but I will find another way. Follow me."

Cyrus opened the door and stepped outside. Maggie followed. Her heart raced when figures in the distance came into view. *Dad? Am I getting rescued?*

"I think you have something of mine," Cyrus said.

"And, I think *you* have something of *mine*." Griffen took a step ahead. "Let's make this exchange and we'll be on our way. I don't want any trouble."

"Trouble? You have already caused me more trouble

than you can imagine. I had a very simple plan for this morning, and you interrupted that. I will make it happen one way or another."

"Dad!" Maggie screamed. "Is that you? You're here!"

"Maggie! It's all going to be okay." Her dad's head inched forward as he looked for her. "Hand over my daughter, and I will do the same."

Cyrus stepped to the side and motioned for his guards to move out of the way. Maggie bolted between them and ran straight into her dad's arms.

"Isn't that sweet," Krado said. He walked over to his father. "Catch you all later. Oh, and tell Santori I'll miss her."

Griffen didn't answer. He loosened his grip on Maggie. "Let's go. We'll continue this reunion once we're safe and out of this place."

"Wait!" Cyrus called. "Where's Santori?"

"She stayed behind to make sure we would get out of here in one piece, and then we'll release her." Griffen looked back at Cyrus. "We needed a guarantee you would stick to your word. Don't worry, we'll get out of your hair now."

Cyrus clenched his fists and punched the door. "Send her back here now! I kept my end of the deal!"

Griffen led the group behind the maid's quarters and found the door to the tunnel entrance. He opened it, and they climbed down the stairs.

"Where are we going?" Maggie asked. "Is Mom down there?"

"No. She didn't make it through the portal in time. This tunnel is how we got to the north side undetected, and it's how we'll get back to the south." When they reached the bottom, Griffen turned to Maggie. "Are you okay? Are you hurt?"

"Yeah, I'm okay." She turned full circle. *Whoa...this place is amazing.*

Peter approached, and Maggie hugged him. "You did it, Peter! You saved me! Thank you!" She stepped back and caught her breath. "Who was that kid? How did you do all this?"

"That was Cyrus' son, Krado. His daughter Santori was down here with her mother, Minka," Peter said.

"Wait...*was* down here?" Griffen asked. He looked around. "Where did Minka and Santori go?"

"They left and told me to stay behind and warn you."

Maggie's eyes drifted to a stone wall with strange writing. She pulled out her journal. *I need to do some investigating down here. There's so much to see.*

⛫

"Cyrus is not going to like this," Larz said.

"Then we need to go now," Griffen said. "If Cyrus realizes Santori is not being released, he'll have his guards searching everywhere to find her. It won't be long before they discover the tunnel entrance. I heard Minka mention something about a corrections team earlier. What was she talking about?"

"A team of thugs that patrol the north side. Everyone fears for their lives. They were the worst of the worst when dark magic thrived here."

"Good thing we didn't run into any of them. You think you can find your way back to Minka's palace? We have a rainbow to catch, and I don't want to miss it."

"I followed Minka close on the way here. I think between the two of us, we should be able to find our way back. As long as those animal statues didn't move."

Griffen frowned. "Okay, let's go." He turned to Peter. "Where's Maggie? She was just here."

"She couldn't have gone far," Peter said. "Maaggiiiee, where are you?"

The air rushed out of Griffen's lungs. "Stay here. I'm going to walk a few feet ahead and see if she's up there."

Maggie sat on the ground, scraping the wall with a rock. The noise blocked the sound of footsteps approaching.

"Maggie! What are you doing? We just got you back. Why did you take off like that without telling anyone?" her dad asked.

"Sorry. I'm investigating. I didn't realize I walked so far away." She ran her fingers over the wall, and dust fell to the ground. "Check out these weird symbols. And this looks like a picture of something, but I have to get this dirt off of it. What do you think this stuff means?" She pressed both hands as hard as she could into the wall to remove more dust. She took out her pen and dug into the tiny cracks that surrounded the shape of something square. "Whoa...it's a book. What's on the front?"

"It looks like a star. Maybe the letter S. But we don't have time to figure it out now."

Peter and the rest of the group approached.

"I should have guessed you left us to play detective," Peter said.

Maggie jumped up at the sight of them. "There's no way I would have missed out on this! It might be the only time we'll ever be able to explore an underground tunnel in another world." She pulled Peter closer to the wall. "Check out what I found."

Peter stared at the symbols and the book on the wall. "The symbols look similar to the ones we saw on Mr. Walric's papers. But I have no idea what that book thing is."

"Yeah, me either. It looks mysterious, though. Mr. Larz, do you know what it is?"

Larz shifted his focus to the wall. His wide eyes fixated on the image.

"Hello! Mr. Larz?" Maggie asked.

"Sorry, no. I have no idea." He studied the carving of the book.

"We've spent enough time down here. We need to go." Griffen ushered them along. "Follow me."

Maggie gathered her things, and the group walked down the dimly lit tunnel, navigating their way back to the south side of the world.

Maggie looked back at the carving on the wall, her eyes lingering until it disappeared.

CHAPTER TWENTY-FIVE

Cyrus' guards stood outside the palace door, waiting for Santori. Inside, Cyrus paced back and forth, loud heaves escaping from his clenched teeth. He'd lost the chance to visit the rainbow, and his daughter's mind was being poisoned by her presumed-dead mother. At least Minka's kindness couldn't sway Krado.

"So, is that woman our mother?" Krado asked.

"Yes. I have an excellent explanation for why I didn't tell you and Santori. A long time ago, my father ruled Zentobia. Your mother's father stole his power and killed him. After he died, I vowed to avenge his death and regain control of Zentobia. I am so close to turning the last star black. Then Zentobia will be mine." He walked to the door. "Where is Santori? She should have been here by now."

"Not sure that will happen. She was pretty enamored with our long-lost mother. I have a feeling she's not coming."

Every muscle in Cyrus's frail body stiffened. "That's not acceptable! I made a deal. They better release her!"

He stuck his oblong head out of the door but didn't hear

a peep. He nudged the guard in the shoulder to get his attention. "Do you see anything?"

"Nothing," the guard responded.

Cyrus slammed his fist into the door so hard he wrapped it in his cape to ease the aching pain. "Round up my staff and have them meet in my office in thirty minutes. Then get the machine ready for nonstop rain." He stormed down the hall and turned back. "And make sure they bring my gold cape."

"What are you going to do?" Krado called.

"What I should have done a long time ago. But first, we'll get Santori back. Follow me. You need to tell me everything that happened last night when those men took you."

CHAPTER TWENTY-SIX

S antori had an easy time convincing Minka to take her back to the south side of Zentobia. This might be the only chance she would have to form a relationship with her mother, and the thought of missing that chance fueled her desperation.

When they arrived at the palace grounds, Santori took in every nook and cranny. She wondered what the people were like who lived in the homes she spotted floating in the distance. *Why don't the homes float where I live? Oh, maybe because it's the dead part of the world.* She glimpsed a few kids playing effortlessly outside. *It would be nice to have friends who can go outside their homes without being scared.* She imagined what it would be like to stroll freely through town without having to watch her back for thieves. In her part of the world, no one would dare steal from Cyrus' daughter, unless they didn't recognize her.

"Come inside. I'll show you where you can stay," Minka said.

What's that amazing smell? Santori took a deep breath to lock in the incredible, unfamiliar fragrance. Bouquets of fresh flowers rested in shiny vases on small tables in each corner of the room. It took a minute for her eyes to adjust to the gold specks of light that gleamed off the walls.

Smooth wood beams hovered in the air with no connection to the ceiling. Her neck hurt from looking up for so long, so she lowered her head. In front of her, the stairs were floating and changing direction.

"I think I'm getting dizzy. What *is* this place? Those beams are hanging on their own, and these stairs...they're all over the place. How's this happening?"

Minka smiled. "These and a few other things around here are courtesy of your grandfather. He used the shifting spell more than he ate dessert, and he loved his sweets. He thought it would be safer if things always changed."

"There's magic here? I thought Zentobians were forbidden to practice magic."

"That's true. I promised my father before he died that I would not pursue its powers. He warned me the danger of magic outweighed its rewards. The one exception is when a threat places southern Zentobia in jeopardy. Let's go. Follow me."

Santori's eyes fixated on the stairs. Adrenaline pulsed through her veins. *I have always wanted to learn magic.* She started to ask Minka more about it but held back.

Minka put her foot on the bottom of the staircase, and it stopped moving. The two walked up together.

When they reached the room at the end of the hall, Minka looked at Santori. "There should be everything you need here and more. I want you to be comfortable, but any time you want to return to your home, just say the word."

"Thank you...Mom. It feels so strange to say it. I've been looking at a videograph of you for so many years, but now I can see you in person and call you Mom. I'm not ready to go home...not yet. I don't know if I'll ever want to go back there. My father lied to me about you and this side of the world for all these years. Krado is obsessed with power, but not me."

"I only hope I can make up for the lost time." Minka opened the door, and they walked inside.

Dolls with long and short hair outfitted in dresses and every piece of clothing imaginable filled straw baskets. Boxes overflowed with unopened toys for every age, and stacks of books on shelves ran up the walls to the ceiling.

"This is incredible!" Santori walked straight over to the dolls and picked up a tall one that had curly red hair and brown eyes. She smoothed down its fluffy yellow dress. "I don't remember ever having a doll. Or any toys like these. I played make-believe most of the time. Thank you for having these things for me."

Tears escaped Santori's eyes and hit the floor. *I can't believe this is real.*

CHAPTER TWENTY-SEVEN

Back in the tunnels, Griffen and Larz tried to navigate their way out. But every direction they went looked the same. Griffen slowed his pace as the group approached an unexpected fork.

He stepped forward to get a closer look. "I don't remember a fork being here before. Larz, do you think the tunnels have shifted?"

"That's what worries me. I heard Minka tell you on our way to the north that the tunnels could shift, and she has no idea where the other paths lead. I don't want to find out. Especially when we could have Cyrus chasing after us at any moment."

"I agree. But we must make a choice. Unless...we split up."

"What do you mean, split up?"

"What if the kids and I go one way and you and your guards go the other? At least one of us will make it back to the south," Griffen said. "Whoever goes the wrong direction could turn around, or at least know someone would rescue them. If we both go the wrong way, we could all get stuck."

Larz walked over to the other guards, and they discussed the option. After a longer-than-necessary conversation, he returned. "Okay, we'll do it. If whoever goes the wrong way is not back at the palace within a few hours, then assemble a search team."

"Yeah, before these tunnels shift again. Which way do you want to go? Should we flip a coin?" Griffen pulled a quarter out of his pocket.

Larz eyed the coin curiously. "What is that?" He touched it.

"That's a quarter," Maggie said. "It's money. We always flip a coin when we have a big decision to make. It has two sides to it: heads or tails. You can either call heads or tails, and if the coin lands on the side you call, you get to choose what you want to do."

"Okay, then I call...*heads*," Larz said.

Griffen flipped the coin in the air, and it landed on tails.

"It's tails. That means we get to decide which way we want to go," Maggie said. She pointed to the path that led to the right. "I think we should go that way."

"You sure you want us to decide, Dad?" Peter asked. "We don't have the best track record with directions. Did you forget we ran away from Minka and ended up in the north side of this world?"

"It's okay. We have a fifty-fifty chance either way. Let's get going. We'll see everyone back at the palace, sooner than later, I hope."

Larz nodded and walked with his guards over to the path on the left.

Griffen and the kids walked right.

Maggie looked back at Larz and his guards as they headed the opposite direction down the tunnel.

"Dad, do you think we're going the right way?" Peter asked. *I really don't want another floor-caving situation. Who knows what else can go wrong down here.*

"I hope so. After what you guys have been through, I'm glad I got here in time to save you. There's no telling what Cyrus would have done, or what he will do now. I don't want any of us to be here to find out."

"Neither do I, and I don't think..." Maggie's voice trailed off. She stopped walking and tugged on Peter's shirt. "Shh! Did you hear that?"

"I didn't hear any..." Soft voices swished through the air like ocean waves, getting louder each second. "Okay, I heard that. Dad, what should we do?"

"Run! Just keep going."

As they ran, Maggie's foot stepped on the back of her dad's shoe. She tripped over her feet and fell. "Ouch! Wait!"

Peter, close behind, caught up and helped her.

"Thanks. I think I hurt my ankle. I don't know if I can run."

Her dad turned back and grabbed one of Maggie's arms. "We have to keep going."

"What about the noises we heard?" she asked, panting.

Griffen cocked his head. "I don't hear them anymore. Let's keep moving."

They picked up their pace until her dad reached an arm out in front to stop her from moving. "Is your ankle okay?"

"I think so, why? What are you doing?" She grabbed her dad's arm. A shadowy figure up ahead cast an eerie appearance on the tunnel walls. "Okay, now I see why you asked. We need to get out of here."

"Shh! Both of you stay here," their dad murmured. "Move to the side of the tunnel. Don't make a sound. I'm going to step ahead."

"Why the heck would you do that?" Peter whispered. "I see the same thing you're seeing, and it doesn't look good."

"Straight ahead might be our only exit." Their dad crept forward. As he inched closer, a scream came from behind him. He swiveled around.

"Maggie! Peter! You okay?" He bolted back and found Chester jumping all over them.

"Dad, it's Chester!" Peter hugged the dog so tightly he yelped. "We chose the right path. We made it back!"

"Chester, what are you doing down here?" their dad asked.

"Minka told me and two guards to wait for you. Where's everyone else?"

"I'm afraid there was a bit of a hiccup. I'll fill you all in when we get to the palace."

Chester's nose scraped the floor, and he escorted them to where two other guards were waiting. They quickly made their way up the stairs and over to Minka's palace.

CHAPTER TWENTY-EIGHT

Inside Minka's palace, guards led Griffen and the kids to Santori's room.

"Whoa...the stairs are floating," Maggie whispered to Peter. *How is that happening? This is so cool.*

Peter nodded and followed Maggie and their dad.

Chatter came from the room at the end of the hall. Griffen peeked his head in. "Ready for visitors?"

"Of course," Minka said. "Glad you guys made it back. This has been quite a day, and a wonderful one at that." She looked at Santori, then turned to Maggie. "It's nice to see you again, Maggie."

"Sorry we ran away from Chester. We just wanted to get home," Maggie said. "We didn't know we went the wrong way until it was too late. Thank you for helping save me. It looks like everyone had an overdue reunion today." She looked over at Santori, ready to ask her a million questions.

"Don't even think about it," Peter said.

"What do you mean? I just want to get to know her." Maggie reached for her backpack. "We need the information for our new case about Zentobia. Don't you want to know what it's like to live in this world?"

"Yes, but I just want to get back to Hailsville." Peter pushed Maggie's hand away from her backpack.

"Hailsville? What are you talking about?" Santori asked.

"No one has told you?" Maggie eyed Minka. "We're from another world and came to Zentobia through a rainbow portal. Now we have to go back home, but hopefully, we can come back to visit and get to know each other."

Santori looked at them, laughing. "Yeah, right, what kind of joke are you guys playing? I just came from the north side of the world, but there *are* no 'other' worlds. *Right?*"

"Actually, they are from another world," Minka said. "It's a long story. I will tell you all about it over dinner tonight."

Santori circled Maggie and Peter, eyeing them from top to bottom.

"Griffen, would you and the kids like to stay for dinner? You won't be able to leave until it starts raining, so you're welcome to stay here until then."

Maggie lifted her heels off the ground, excitement brewing. *Nothing this fun ever happens in Hailsville.*

"Thank you. That sounds good." Griffen walked closer to Minka. "I need to fill you in on what happened in the tunnels."

"What do you mean?"

Griffen explained the fork they'd encountered. "I don't know where Larz and the guards ended up."

Minka frowned. "I have never come across something like that."

"Yeah, and we heard footsteps and voices too," Maggie added.

"Do you think it was Cyrus?" Minka asked Griffen. "Could he have followed you down there?"

"I don't know. But if it was him, he probably would have tried to capture us. Unless he wanted to follow us to find out the location of the exit. If Larz isn't back within a couple hours, he said you should send help."

"I'll deploy a few guards down there now to investigate and see if they can figure out what you heard. We need to find Larz before the tunnels shift." Minka gestured for her guards to head to the tunnels. "If Cyrus found them, we could all be in danger."

Griffen turned to Maggie. "How much does Cyrus know about the rainbow?"

"I gave him a quick version of it. But he wanted me to take him there this morning. I think he wants to go through the portal and get all the people in Hailsville to become his followers. He mentioned a factory where he is making something special." Her eyes grew wider. "Oh no! With all the excitement, I forgot to tell you this. I saw a bunch of people he captured. He's making them work for him in that factory. Dad, we have to get them out of there! They looked really sad, and their clothes were all torn."

The color escaped Minka's face. "A factory? More like a laboratory. There's only one thing he could be working on."

"What is it?" Griffen asked.

"When the excess rain first started, I sent Talia over to the north to investigate. She got there and back without being seen and found the machine he's using to control the weather in a laboratory." She walked over to a photo of her palace on the wall. "But with the right technology, that machine can change the stars. If he's trying to turn our last gold star black, then he could resurrect dark magic and control the minds of everyone in this world. We have to stop him."

"And we have to free those people he's making work there," Maggie said. "I want to help."

"I know you do, but don't you think you've been through enough?" Griffen asked.

"I'm the only one who knows where he's keeping the prisoners. You need my detective skills." Maggie looked at her dad with her best puppy-dog face that always won him over.

He turned to Minka. "There've been some people in Hailsville who have gone missing. Maybe they went through the rainbow portal by accident and ended up being captured by Cyrus. I planned to go back to Hailsville and alert my sheriff. But now, with what Maggie said about those prisoners, and your world being in danger, I want to help. I couldn't have gotten Maggie back without you. Let me return the favor."

"You're not seriously thinking of sending Maggie back there, are you, Dad?" Peter asked.

Before Griffen could respond, a guard walked in and interrupted. "Minka, Mr. Walric is here. He wants to see if Griffen is back with the kids. Should I send him in?"

"Yes, please do. Thank you."

Mr. Walric walked into the room with a spring in his step.

Maggie ran up to him. "Mr. Drop! I didn't know if I would ever see you again. Oh, and Peter and I believe you now."

Mr. Walric smiled. "It's good to see you too Maggie. I'm glad Peter helped your dad and Minka find you. My actual name is Mr. Walric. When I got to Hailsville, I forgot my name, so I came up with Drop."

"I like Mr. Drop better anyway. I hope I can still call you that."

He nodded. "Of course."

Griffen walked over and put a hand on Mr. Walric's shoulder. "Good to see you. Thanks again for your help in getting me here. I don't know what would have happened without you."

"You're welcome. I just wanted to come by to see if the kids were okay and find out what you'll do next."

"We were hoping to head home, but something has come up." He looked at Minka.

"My fear about Cyrus being up to no good was correct," Minka said. She filled Mr. Walric in on Cyrus's plan.

Mr. Walric stumbled on his words. "We...we can't let that happen. There would be no happiness left in this world under Cyrus's control. It would be chaos."

"Exactly. That's why I'm going to help free the prisoners so they can't work in the factory anymore," Maggie said. "Part of being a good detective is helping people when you know they're in trouble."

"There is a way we can get them out," Minka said.

"What is it?" Maggie ran to her side.

"I can send over Brit. She's my secret weapon. If anyone can get in there and free those prisoners, it's her." She looked at Griffen. "You up for another visit to the north?"

"Yes! He's up for it." Maggie tugged on her dad's arm. "And so am I."

"Fine. Let's go free some prisoners," Griffen said.

Minka walked over to the phone. "I'll call Brit and fill her in."

CHAPTER TWENTY-NINE

L arz stopped in the middle of the tunnel corridor and reached down to tighten his shoe. He and the guards had walked for miles. Every time he thought they'd reached the end, the tunnel took them in another direction. There were no floating animals anywhere, and the temperature kept dropping. The sound of whispering voices came out of nowhere, and Larz didn't have time to direct his team to turn around.

"Shh!" he whispered to the other two guards. "Do you hear that? It sounds like voices."

One guard, Leo, replied, "I do. I don't think it's Griffen, Maggie, and Peter."

"Neither do I. Stay close and move to the side of the tunnel. I think we need to turn around. My gut tells me if we keep going, we might not like what we find."

Leo nodded. The other guard, Cafferdy, spoke up. "Why don't I see where this tunnel leads while you two turn back? If I don't return in a few hours, you can send someone for me. It might be our only chance to find out what else is down here and where these tunnels go."

The voices grew louder.

"That idea might have worked before we heard the voices, but we all have to go now. Run!" Larz yelled.

The guards ran down the tunnel, not realizing the voices came from in front of them, not behind them. They came to a halt, encountering the one thing they had been trying to avoid. Cyrus stood straight ahead, looking right back at them with a row of guards at his side.

"Isn't this perfect timing?" Cyrus sneered. "Guards, get those *guards*, if that's what you call yourselves." He let out a daunting chuckle. "We found the tunnels, and now we found something else that belongs to Minka. My leverage is growing by the minute."

Two of Cyrus' guards set their torches down and grabbed Larz, Leo, and Cafferdy and tied up their hands.

Cyrus jumped back when the flame from one torch almost lit his gold cape on fire. "Idiots!" He pushed the cape behind his shoulders.

"Minka is too smart for your so-called leverage," Larz said, squirming his hands up and down inside the rope. "Everyone could live in peace if you weren't so greedy."

Cyrus stepped closer to Larz. He pulled out a blade and swung it like a pendulum in front of his darkened face. "Greed? What do you know about greed? I earned everything I have, and I will earn more! Minka broke our agreement, and now she has Santori. That is not how things will end. I will see to it, and you three *gentlemen* will help me."

Cyrus took a step back, and his sharp blade glistened as it caught the glow of the torch flames. With a wave of his other hand, he signaled his guards to follow behind with the prisoners. They all headed down the dreary path, deeper into the tunnels.

The shallow breathing of Larz and his guards echoed between the four walls in the holding room inside Cyrus' palace. Leo and Cafferdy were slumped against the wall, drifting in and out of sleep. Larz sat upright, trying to cover his nose and mouth with his shirt. The room smelled of wet paint and stale dust. He stood and nudged the other guards with his shoe.

"Wake up. We need to get our story straight," Larz began, "so when Cyrus comes to question us, we're all on the same page. Remember, no one can tell him how the rainbow portal works. If he wants to get to the south side of the world through the tunnels, we're all starting from scratch, because they have probably shifted by now. That will buy us some time."

They nodded. The door swung open. Cyrus and two guards walked into the room.

The smell of fresh paint flooded the air, causing Larz to gag. "If you're doing some remodeling, I know a tradesman who uses paint that won't give you an asthma attack."

"Make jokes if you will, but you won't be making them for much longer." Cyrus slammed his fist against the wall. "First, you will take me to Minka. I am going to get my daughter back. Second, if you live long enough, you can either join my army of guards in the north or become my slaves."

Larz shook his head. Leo and Cafferdy stood in the corner, tapping their feet to the fast-paced sound of their breaths.

"And if we refuse to take you back through the tunnels?" Larz asked.

"I will show you what will happen." Cyrus pulled out a

knife, walked over to Larz, and waved it like an airplane in front of his head. He signaled his guards to grab the prisoners and head toward the door. "Look down this hall. I fill these rooms with my slaves. They are not here because I went out and captured them. I am not a monster. They are here because they did not do what I asked of them. This is their punishment."

They walked into the dark hallway. Cyrus used the blade to flick a switch on the wall, and a disturbing vision came into view. On one side of the hallway, rows of rooms filled with prisoners went on as far as the eye could see. On the other side, additional rooms were being built where workers were applying fresh coats of paint to the walls.

"There's a room for each of you," Cyrus said, grinning. "As you can see, I'm expanding my resources. Once I take over the south side of the world, there might be a few who resist. Follow me; let me show you what could be your new home for a while, a *long* while."

Cyrus wrapped his scrawny fingers around the knife several times before putting it back into a holder hanging from his belt. The group walked down the hall.

Larz turned to peer into the rooms and squinted. Some were empty, while men, women, and children, who all looked tired and lonely, occupied others.

"This is insanity," Larz said. "How long have these people been here?"

"They all have different sentences, depending on their disobedience." Cyrus stopped in front of a room where a man slept on a mattress. "This man...his name is Lupo. My corrections team caught him trying to escape to the south. He is paying for his crime by working in my factory." Cyrus pulled out his knife and held it in front of Larz's head. He stepped forward a few feet to the room next to Lupo. The others followed. A woman and a child were inside the room. The woman read a book to the child.

A wave of sadness came over Larz, which quickly turned into anger. He clenched his hands into fists. "How generous of you to give them a book."

"As I said before, I'm not a monster," Cyrus began, "unless someone is deserving of such treatment. We caught this woman telling tales to a group of people about the south. She will serve less time here and have the privilege of having her child with her. She received the book for good behavior." He put the knife back into the holder on his belt.

Larz rolled his eyes. "I've seen enough. I get the point."

Cyrus walked up to Larz, inches from his face. "Good. Let's get going. I don't want to waste any more time."

"Neither do I." Larz looked over at Leo and Cafferdy and turned his body sideways. He put his hand in front of his chest, signaling he would attack Cyrus. With the blink of an eye, he launched behind Cyrus and put his head in a chokehold. Cyrus gagged, clutching for air. He grabbed the knife out of Cyrus' belt, but it slipped out of his sweaty hand and onto the floor. Leo leaped forward to grab the knife, but one of Cyrus' guards jumped on top of him, bringing them both to the slippery floor. Leo shrieked in pain and squirmed his injured body forward to reach the knife. His fingertips extended further, gripping the blade. He hoisted his way up from underneath the hefty guard and placed the knife into Larz's hand, still wrapped tightly around Cyrus' scrawny neck.

Cyrus yelped. The knife grazed his skin. Blood dripped down his neck. He glared at the guards. "Look what you've done."

"No, Cyrus, it's what you have done, which you will pay for," Larz said. "Let's move. All of you. Back into the holding room or your boss won't live to see the final coat of paint on these walls." Leo and Cafferdy grabbed the other two guards and shoved them back down the hall and into the holding room. "Leo, grab the rope on the floor and tie them all up."

Larz released Cyrus and pushed him to the back of the room with his other guards. Leo grabbed the rope and wrapped it tightly around their wrists, then joined Larz and Cafferdy by the door.

Cyrus twisted his hands up and down inside the rope. "You'll never make it out of here."

"Watch me." Larz and the guards exited the room and locked the door behind them. "Let's get out of here."

"What about the people in these rooms?" Cafferdy asked.

"We don't have time to find the keys right now. Our best option is to get out of here and head back to Minka's palace. We need to warn her that Cyrus is out for blood, and then we can come up with a plan."

They made their way down the long hall, avoiding the faces of the prisoners behind the walls.

CHAPTER THIRTY

S antori and Maggie sat on the couch in the corner of the room, comparing notes about their worlds.

Maggie listened intently until the clunking sound of boots caught her attention. A woman, dressed like the other guards, entered. *Whoa...she looks like a bodybuilder.* Maggie kept her eyes glued to the stranger.

The woman walked over to Minka and Griffen, who were looking at a floor plan of Cyrus's palace spread out on a desk.

Maggie listened on the sidelines.

"I got here as fast as I could," the woman said to Minka.

"Thank you, Brit. This is Griffen and his son, Peter. Maggie is over there." Minka pointed to the couch. "She is the one who alerted us to the prisoners."

"Who's the other girl?" Brit asked. "She looks familiar. Wait...is that...?"

"It's Santori. I'll fill you in later." Minka showed Brit the floor plan. "You'll need this. Griffen can go over everything with you on the way there. We'll outfit everyone with flying shoes, and then you can head out."

Brit took the floor plan, glanced at it, and tucked it away into the side pocket of her pants. "Who's everyone? I thought it was just me and a few of my men."

"I'm going to go over there with you, and we're bringing Maggie," Griffen said. "I need to look for a few people from Hailsville that Cyrus might be holding."

Brit scrunched her face. "Sorry, but that place is too dangerous for a kid and her father."

Minka put a hand on Brit's shoulder. "Griffen is doing us a favor, and his daughter knows where Cyrus is holding the prisoners. We could use their help. Besides, he works for the police department in his world, so he has some training."

"Fine, but the kid stays outside the palace."

"I couldn't agree with you more," Griffen said. "I'll go in with you."

"Why don't we bring Walric to keep an eye on the kid?" Brit asked.

"That works for me," Griffen said. He turned to Minka. "You okay watching Peter while we're gone?"

"Of course."

"Can we get back to the flying shoes for a minute?" Griffen asked. "Not that I'm opposed to flying across the world, but why don't we just take the tunnels?"

Minka laughed. "It wasn't that long ago that we fell through a floor in them, and Larz is still lost down there. I think flying is safer right now. Brit knows a back way to get past any sky guards."

"Yep." Brit pulled her long dark hair into a tight pony-tail. "Let's go get fitted for flying shoes."

Maggie raced over. "Did I hear you say 'flying shoes?'"

"Hey, Maggie, I'm Brit. You heard right. We're all going to fly to the north."

Maggie jumped up and down. *I can't believe I get to fly! This is going to be so cool!*

Griffen gathered Mr. Walric and Peter to fill them in on the plan.

"I really don't want to stay here," Peter said. "But I really don't want to go there either. This is not an easy choice."

"It's a good thing you don't have to make one, then, because you're not going. There's no need for both my kids to risk their lives. I'm not happy about Maggie going, but she will stay outside the palace with Mr. Walric. I'll see you when we get back." Griffen headed to the door with the others.

Peter walked to the back of the room and took a seat.

Santori approached him. She unwound her hair from the bun on top of her head and let it fall against her face.

"You jealous your sister gets to fly across the world and save some people?" She sat next to Peter on the floor.

"No. I already saved Maggie."

"Maggie told me all about Hailsville and your lives there. Sounds like Hailsville could use a little excitement. I was thinking how fun it would be to go back there with you and check it out for myself."

What's she up to? "No way. That's not a good idea." He stood and faced her. "I mean...you have a lot going on here right now. Don't you want to help your mom?"

"I do. But it sounds like Maggie needs a little help too. You know, making friends and all. I'm good at that. Look at us. We're becoming friends."

We are not becoming friends. "I would say more like

acquaintances. I don't know you well enough yet to be your friend."

Santori grinned. "Well, then, we'll just have to get to know each other better."

CHAPTER THIRTY-ONE

Larz and the guards escaped the palace and made their way through the outskirts of northern Zentobia. Not much had changed since Larz had last been there. Several tall, broken buildings survived in the distance, probably still occupied by workers in Cyrus' debt, he thought.

Clusters of little huts peeked through the lifeless fields. Soon, their owners would be tucked safely inside for the night. Danger always brewed after dark, as desperate dwellers made it their hobby to steal from those more fortunate.

Every so often, the loud crunching sound of dead branches under Larz's shoes startled him, and he imagined they must be remnants from the once-plentiful Tigwat trees.

"Do you think we're close?" Cafferdy asked.

"Not much closer than we were when you asked me five minutes ago," Larz said. Something ahead caught his attention. A group of young kids played in the field. "I want to talk to those kids."

"Are you crazy?" Cafferdy said. "I thought you wanted to remain out of sight. Why do you want to talk to them?"

"I want to find out what the people here know about the south. It might be useful for Minka."

Cafferdy shook his head and looked at Leo. Leo frowned. The three walked closer to the small group of boys, not much older than eleven or twelve. The ball they were playing with flew past their reach, and Larz caught it.

"Hi there. I think I caught your ball," Larz said to the boys.

"Are you one of Cyrus's guards?" asked a boy. "We finished our chores and are just getting some exercise."

"No, I'm not a guard. I just like to dress like one." Larz smiled and tried to make small talk. The boys laughed, and he along with them. "I'm wondering, have you boys ever been to the south side of the world?"

The laughter stopped. The boys looked at each other. One of them spoke up. "There is no south side of the world. It doesn't exist anymore."

"Sure it does." He raised his eyebrows. "Where did you hear it doesn't exist?"

One of the boys backed up, turned, and ran away.

"We're not supposed to talk about the south," another boy said. "Don't you know that? We'll get captured. We have to go."

The rest of the boys ran off, leaving Larz, Leo, and Cafferdy on their own.

"Did you hear that?" Larz asked. "Do you think they believe the south doesn't exist, or are they spreading Cyrus's propaganda? Either way, it's not good. Let's get going. We still have some ground to cover."

The three started moving again, walking in silence until

a shuffling sound came from nearby. A group of owls circled directly above, staring down at them.

"Quick, behind this tree," Larz said. The three jumped behind the ragged tree. "Get down."

"Why are we hiding from a group of owls behind a dead tree that's barely giving us any coverage?" Leo asked.

"We are on the north side, that's why," Larz said. "Those owls are not the same kind we have on our side. Let's just stay here until they pass, and then we'll keep going."

The owls circled overhead for a few minutes, then hovered in place.

"Great, we will never get out of here," Leo whispered.

Larz put his finger up to his mouth. "Shh!"

The owls scattered and flew away.

"That can't be good." Larz pointed north. "If I had to guess, I would say those owls belong to Cyrus. They're probably on their way back to him now."

"You think they saw us?" Cafferdy asked, looking up at the dead tree. "I think I answered my own question. They probably saw us."

"Let's go," Larz said. "We can't let Cyrus get to Minka before we do."

Cyrus and his guards were screaming for twenty minutes in the holding room before another set of guards found them tied up on the floor.

"It took you long enough," Cyrus complained as his hands were untied. "My prisoners escaped. They will pay for this once we capture them again. Now move!"

The group hurried down the hallway and up to the main floor, where they encountered Krado sitting on the floor, snacking on a tigwat. Three bags of overstuffed luggage and a backpack filled with tons of food rested at his feet.

"Finally, you show up," Krado said to his father. He stood, chomping on the fruit. Juice splattered all over Cyrus's angry face. "I've been waiting for almost a half hour. Are we leaving now?"

Cyrus wiped the juice out of his eyes and looked at Krado's bags. "Some things tied me up for a bit. Where do you think you're going with all that stuff? We're not moving to the south. We're just going to retrieve Santori and take care of some business. Put all of that away."

Krado groaned. "I'll need this if we get delayed or something unexpected comes up."

"The only thing that will come up is you not going with me if you don't get rid of it." He walked away, his guards close behind. "Be ready to leave here in five minutes."

Krado kicked one bag feverishly. "Ouch!" He screamed down the hall at his father. "Fine! Have it your way. When we run out of stuff, don't say I didn't warn you."

He took a few things out of the three bags and stuffed as much as he could into the backpack. He brought the other bags back to his room, and when he returned, a group of owls were rummaging through his backpack.

"Hey Screech. What are you doing here?"

"We spotted some runaways headed south and thought Cyrus might want to know about them," Screech said. "Where is he?"

Krado raised his brows. "Runaways? What did they look like?"

"They looked like guards, but not any of Cyrus' guards." Screech flew up and down.

"Okay, thanks. I'll tell my father. You can be on your way now."

Screech and the other owls flew away toward the palace exit. Krado straightened up his bag.

Cyrus walked up to Krado and asked, "What was Screech doing here?"

"His daily rounds," Krado lied. "Nothing to report."

"Good. Let's head to the tunnels." Cyrus waved his hands erratically. "We need to make up for lost time."

After exiting the palace, he led them to the spot where he'd found the tunnel entrance. He moved the scattered shrubs to look for the door. "It's gone!" He shuffled around the shrubs madly. "Where's the door?"

His guards looked too but came up empty-handed.

"I guess we'll have to fly there," Krado said to Cyrus, who, like a madman, kicked and scraped the ground until brown dirt ran up his legs.

"More delays! Back to the palace for our gear," Cyrus began, "and put your flying shoes on full speed. We'll make up the time in the air." He clenched his fists at his side. "Before we go, I need to make a detour to my lab and make sure we're on track for the rain."

CHAPTER THIRTY-TWO

At the back door of Minka's palace, Maggie fiddled with her flying shoes. Their silver laces melded together once they reached her ankles. "These are a little loose. Will they fall off?"

"No. They'll conform to your feet once you're in the air. Just leave them, and I promise they'll work." Brit effortlessly clasped together the wide strap on her shoes. "Just remember the lesson I gave you about midair flight, and whatever you do, just focus and keep going."

Griffen grabbed Maggie's hand. "We've got this." He turned to Brit. "We're ready. I want to get back before any chance of rain so we can catch that portal and get home."

"Then it's a good thing I scored the upgraded shoes," Brit said.

She explained that for the past year, a team of skilled engineers had worked nonstop on a new technology aimed at increasing the speed on flying shoes. Not quite ready to release to Zentobians, the technology would make traveling to and from work much faster and more efficient. "I convinced the lead engineer to install the technology into our shoes, but we can't tell anyone. Let's go." Brit took off. Mr. Walric followed.

Maggie held her dad's hand, and they lifted off the ground. Her stomach dropped as the speed increased. The smell from the silver flames leaving the shoes reminded her of fumes from the gas station near her home in Hailsville. "This is amazing and scary, and I can't believe this is happening." Below, Zentobia got smaller and smaller as they flew higher. *My body is so light up here. Am I in space? Doubt it, the sky's still blue. I have to try this on my own.* She released her hand from her dad's, and her body wobbled from side to side. Cold, fresh air blew swiftly against her face, causing her to squint.

Brit flew next to her. "Just keep it steady. You'll get used to the wind. Focus on moving straight ahead."

"This is a lot harder than it looks." Maggie's legs twisted, and she circled around. *Yikes! This is crazy!* "Oh no! I can't balance. Someone help!"

Brit grabbed her arm. "You've got this."

I can do it. Maggie steadied her breathing and held her hands out to her sides. "It's working. I'm flying! Woohoo!"

They flew in silence the rest of the way. Maggie practiced tricks but kept losing her balance. As they approached the palace, Brit signaled to the group to land on the side of the building behind a set of dead trees.

Oh no. I forgot how to slow down. "Yikes! Dad! I can't slow these things down!"

"Tap your right foot twice," Brit yelled from the ground.

Maggie tapped her foot inches from the ground, and she landed on her hands and knees. "Ouch! That was the worst landing ever."

Her dad ran to her side. "You okay?"

"Yep." She stood. "I'll stick the landing next time."

Brit surveyed the area. "Maggie, you sure the location is down a set of stairs?"

"Yep, I remember walking down to where they took me."

"Okay then. Stay back here with Walric. Is everyone ready?"

They all nodded.

One guard paced back and forth along the side door to the palace. Brit stretched out her muscular legs. "Here we go." Her petite body sprang forward and walked up to the guard by the palace door. "Hey, do you know where I can find a bathroom around here?"

Caught by surprise, the guard didn't have time to react. Brit's weapon, neatly tucked into her hand, edged its way out like a sword and launched a sleeping dart at him. The dart hit him in the neck. "I still got my aim." She turned back to the group, which was watching from behind the trees, and signaled for Griffen to join her.

Griffen caught up to Brit at the entrance.

"What's she doing with you?" Brit asked.

Griffen whipped his head around.

Maggie stood right behind him. "Hi, Dad."

"Maggie! Get back over with Mr. Walric. This is too dangerous."

"But there is someone inside I need to make sure gets out. I talked to him when I was there. He thinks he's been here for a year. I want to help him."

"We're running out of time," Brit said. "She's going to have to come."

Griffen clenched his jaw. "Stay right behind me and do *not* wander off."

They entered the palace and made their way down the dismal hall to the winding staircase that led to the floor below. No one emerged from the dark corners in the eerily quiet building.

"This is too easy so far." Brit stood at the top of the staircase and peered down. She looked back at Griffen. "I can't see what's down there, but we'll overtake anyone that stands in the way of releasing the prisoners." She treaded lightly down the stairs.

Griffen and Maggie followed close behind. The quiet chatter of voices from below became louder. Maggie itched her nose from the smell of paint, which grew stronger as they descended.

Brit stopped short before reaching the bottom.

Two armed guards stood watch, each wearing a belt with rows of keys hanging from a loop.

"Those have got to be the keys. There's only two of them. I'll go at them with the sleeping darts." Brit turned to Griffen. "You grab the keys and open the rooms. Once everyone is out, they can follow us to the exit."

Griffen nodded.

She crept down the remaining steps and leaped forward, weapon in hand. Her first shot hit the guard on the left in the neck. He put his hand up to pull out the dart but immediately fell to the ground. Before she could direct her fire to the second guard, he pulled his weapon out and aimed it toward her.

Griffen jumped in front and shot a sleeping dart at him. It landed on his shoulder, and he tumbled sideways to the floor.

"That was close," Griffen said.

"Thanks for covering me. Now get the keys."

He ran over to the guard's limp body and shuffled through the keys on his belt, trying to get them loose. A heaving tug pulled them free, and he gave half of them to Brit.

Maggie grabbed the rest of the keys from her dad's hand. "I want to help."

He nodded. "We'll do it together."

Brit looked back at them. "You two start at that end of the corridor, and I'll take this one. I'll direct the prisoners to the stairs to wait until we're ready to go."

One by one, Maggie put the keys inside the locks and twisted to open the holding room doors. "We're here to set you free." When she came to the last room, a tall, thin man wobbled out.

The man stared into Maggie's eyes. "I recognize your voice."

"I'm Maggie. I think I was in the room next to you. I told you my family would come for me, and I came back for you and everyone else."

Tears streamed down his face. "Thank you for saving us."

Dozens of prisoners stepped outside their holding rooms, looking down the hall at each other. Whispers filled the corridor. Joy spread through the air.

"That's the last one," Brit said. "Griffen, you stay at the back with Maggie. I'll head to the front. Let's get them out of here."

The large group scurried past the sleeping guards and up the stairs. At the top, Brit gave a thumbs-up signal to everyone, and they ran down the empty hallway, the side door of the palace within sight.

Before they made it there, a team of owls intersected them. "What do we have here?" Screech scowled.

Maggie hid behind one of the prisoners. *If that owl sees me, we're toast!* She lowered her head.

Brit looked over at Griffen and winked. "We're moving the prisoners during the remodel. Cyrus wants another coat of paint on the walls."

Screech flew up and down and then sideways.

"How come I've never seen you around here?" The owl's wings flapped wildly.

"I'm new. Cyrus beefed up security, and we're in charge of the prisoners."

"There's been a lot going on around here lately. Perhaps Cyrus did add you on to his security."

"That is exactly why he added us. You're right. You must know Cyrus pretty well. The last time I saw him, he mentioned he wanted to talk to you."

The owl scowled. "Did he?"

Brit and the prisoners moved forward, slithering their way around the owls.

Maggie moved to the back, trying to blend in with the group. *This owl is suspicious. We need a distraction.* The heavy breathing of the prisoner next to her caught her attention.

"Yes," Brit began, "he's upstairs in his office. Let him know the painters are ready to start the final coat. I'm sure he'll appreciate you giving him the message." Her slow stride turned into a power walk.

Maggie turned to the man next to her, whose silver hair covered his gaunt face. "Start to cough. Loud. That will distract the owl."

The man nodded. His deep coughs echoed throughout the hall.

Brit looked in his direction. "That man needs medical attention. Let's go."

"Wait! You didn't tell me your name," Screech said.

"Of course. It's Brit. Cyrus and I go way back." She quickly waved goodbye.

In the back of the line, Maggie thanked the prisoner. "Oh, and you can stop coughing now."

Her dad turned to the prisoner. "Are you okay? That was a pretty nasty cough."

"Yes, it was her idea," the man said as he pointed to Maggie. "I'm happy to help. I don't get to do much of anything anymore. That all stopped when I got to this forsaken world."

Her dad's jaw dropped. "What do you mean? Where did you come from?"

"You wouldn't believe me if I told you. I already tried to convince that Cyrus guy I'm not from here, but it did me no good."

"Are you from Hailsville?"

The man's dark face faded, and a small smile formed. "How did you know that? There's two others from there too, but we've had no chance to get out of here."

"Looks like your luck has changed. When we get outside and away from here, point out the other two so we can get you all back home."

The man nodded. His breath quickened with excitement.

The encounter with the owls caused an unexpected delay. They finally reached the side door, and Brit opened it with force.

"Let's go." The prisoners followed Brit outside, where the guard's limp body still rested. "Once we're far enough away, take shelter in your homes or somewhere safe."

Cheers of joy erupted.

"Shh! You're not in the clear yet. Let's all get out of here. Move along," Brit said.

The group whispered "thank you" and "you're our hero" as they ran, walked, skipped, and sprinted by Maggie, Brit, and Griffen, who had saved them from a life of misery inside the palace.

Three stray prisoners walked up to Brit. She turned to Griffen. "Who are *they?*"

"Long story, but the short of it is I need to bring them back with me."

"Okay then. Let's get going." Brit opened the bag she'd left with Mr. Walric and pulled out flying shoes. "Never leave home without extras." She turned to the freed prisoners."Put these on. No time for a flying lesson."

Maggie landed first at the back door of Minka's palace. *Nailed it!* She ran inside looking for Peter. *I can't wait to tell him what happened.*

A guard greeted her in the hallway. "Hello, Miss Maggie. Your brother is in Minka's office. They're all anxiously waiting for your return."

"Thank you!" She tried to fly down the hall, but the shoes didn't work. *I wonder why they don't work here. Maybe I have to be outside. Ugh, I really want to show Peter.*

After reuniting with her brother, Minka, and Santori, Maggie told them about the rescue. "It was amazing to put the key in each door to free them."

Griffen entered the room with the three people from Hailsville. "We did it. They're all free."

"Maggie just filled us in. Thank you all for everything," Minka said. "You gave me my daughter back and saved so many lives."

He walked to Minka. "You're welcome. But it's not over." Griffen pointed to the window in the office. "Cyrus remains a threat. He's still controlling the weather.

Speaking of which, it's raining. I think we can try to go home now."

"Okay. At least we stalled his plans for now. He can't change the last star without the prisoners to work on that machine," Minka said. "Our only hope is if the people in the north can avoid his corrections team long enough for us to figure out a plan."

"Why can't his guards just work on the machine?"

"Because the guards monitor everyone around the clock. If he takes them off the streets for any amount of time, people might rebel. Let's gather everyone, and we'll walk to the rainbow together."

CHAPTER THIRTY-THREE

On the way to the rainbow, Maggie and Santori spoke effortlessly about the challenges of making friends and growing up alone in their worlds. Maggie heard bits from her dad and Minka's conversation about Zentobia and hoped to find out more details later. Peter bounced between the two discussions, contributing his two cents now and then. Mr. Walric tagged along in the background with the three people from Hailsville.

"I wish you didn't have to go so soon," Santori said to Maggie. "You're the first chance I have at making a genuine friend. The girls I meet just want to be friends with me for who my father is. And he likes it that way. But I never really get to know anyone, and they don't get to know the real me. Here, I want to give you something to remember me in case we never see each other again." Santori unfastened a chain link from her wrist. "It's a friendship bracelet. I wear two of them. I am giving you one."

"Wow, that's so nice! Thank you!" Maggie held out her arm. "I love it!" She felt sorry for Santori. They were very similar in a lot of ways. She longed for a genuine friend in

Hailsville, and she spent more time honing her detective skills than she did playing with the kids at school.

"Maybe I could come back to Hailsville with you? Just for a little while?" Santori whispered. She clasped the bracelet closed. "I know we would have a blast."

That's tempting, but no way. You just found out your mother is alive, and your father is an evil villain who would come to Hailsville and enslave everyone if he found out you went with us. Before Maggie could reply, the bright, bold rainbow jumped out in front of them.

"There it is!" Maggie said.

Maggie remembered everything about the rainbow, and her eagerness and apprehension to go through it made her stomach twist in knots.

"I'm afraid you don't have much time," Minka told Griffen. "The rain could stop at any minute. I hope we get to see each other again under more pleasant circumstances. There is still so much we can learn from each other. And Peter, Maggie, don't go jumping through this rainbow again."

"That won't be a problem," Peter said. "This adventure was more than enough excitement for a lifetime. You should come to Hailsville, though. There are no talking animals, but we've got tons of rain and fog to win you over."

Minka laughed and hugged everyone as they made their way closer to the rainbow's end. Santori, still holding Maggie's hand, followed.

"Thanks for everything," Griffen said. "I hope Larz gets back okay. I would like to have a talk with him if I come back. I have a few suggestions for his security team to tighten things up a bit."

Mr. Walric waved a last goodbye and pulled Minka aside to chat.

"I think we should try something different this time and all go into the rainbow together," Griffen said to Maggie and Peter. "I don't want to take any chances of someone getting left behind." He turned to the others. "As soon as we walk in, follow right behind us."

"Good idea," Maggie said. She turned to Santori and hugged her. "I'll miss you!"

The group moved closer. All three bent down and stepped inside the ray of colors. A buzz radiated in the air.

"Do you hear that?" Maggie asked. "It's the same noise we heard last time we stepped into the rainbow. I think it's going to work."

As they moved in, a tug on Maggie's arm momentarily pulled her in the wrong direction. She turned back to see Santori by her side. She had linked the friendship bracelets together with a small lock when she hugged Maggie goodbye.

"Santori! What are you doing?" Maggie asked. "Get out of here now before it's too late!"

Those were the last words Maggie spoke before they were swept away.

<hr />

Mr. Walric wiped the rain from his brow as he and Minka stood near the rainbow. He shared old stories about her father, but she only heard every other word. She wished Griffen, Peter, and Maggie could stay in Zentobia longer.

Where is Santori? She turned around to see Santori's body disappear into the rainbow.

"No!" Minka yelled. She ran over to the rainbow. "Santori, stop!"

Her call came too late. The portal swept her away.

Minka's scream alarmed the guards, and one of them ran over to check on her.

"Renault, Santori went into the rainbow, and now she's gone," Minka whimpered. "You have to go through the portal before it closes and bring her back."

"But if it doesn't stay open," Renault began, "we would be stuck there. What about the memory potion so I can get us back?"

"If you find Santori, she'll be with Griffen. He'll know what to do. Get over there and bring her back before Cyrus stops the rain, or worse, figures out he can go through the portal."

Renault nodded. Without hesitation, he jumped into the rainbow and was on his way to Hailsville.

Mr. Walric approached Minka, but she waved him away. *Why would Santori want to leave so soon after our reunion?* She tried to keep her composure and held back the tears. The hope of having her daughter in her life slipped away.

CHAPTER THIRTY-FOUR

Maggie sprang to her feet and looked around. Mr. Winter's house appeared in the distance. *We made it home!* A few feet away, she spotted Santori trying to lift her head. *Santori? Oh no.* Peter's mumbles caught her attention. She ran over to him, kneeled, and shook his arm. "Peter! Peter! Wake up! Are you okay?" She reached out and grabbed his shoulders to pull him up. His limp body fell back to the ground.

"Maggie, is that you?" Peter said, groggy. "Did we make it home? Is Dad here?" He smiled as he pulled himself up from the ground. His eyes landed on Santori, and the grin disappeared.

"I don't believe this." He pointed to Santori. "What is *she* doing here?"

Maggie stood and turned toward Santori. She vaguely remembered a tugging on her arm and seeing Santori standing next to her when they entered the rainbow in Zentobia. She looked down and wrapped her hand around the empty spot on her wrist where the chain-link bracelet used to be.

"She must have linked our bracelets together with some kind of lock," Maggie blurted.

"That was sneaky and dangerous," her dad said, interrupting their conversation. "I'm not happy about this."

"Dad!" Maggie yelled. She jumped into his arms and squeezed him tight. "I had no idea. I promise."

"Okay. We need to wake up Santori and get home, because it's only a matter of time before Cyrus figures out how to get here. We have to be ready." He looked around for the others, who followed behind them. "I'm going to check on those guys and make sure they can get home okay. I'll be right back."

Maggie and Peter walked over to Santori.

Maggie bent over, shook her arm, and whispered softly, "Wake up."

Peter pushed Maggie out of the way. "Wake up, you sneaky rascal!"

"Why are you yelling at her?"

Peter threw his hands in the air. "Why do you think? Because she had no right to come back with us. Now her psycho father will follow her, and he'll probably bring her crazy brother. I just want this to be over and get things back to normal."

Maggie looked up at her dad as he approached, and he put a hand on her shoulder.

Santori squirmed below. She slowly lifted her head and pushed her hands under her shoulders to inch her way off the ground. "Whoa...where am I? This doesn't look like Zentobia." She stood slowly and spotted Maggie standing next to her.

Peter said something, but Maggie covered his mouth with her hand before he could get a nasty word out.

"Welcome to Hailsville," Maggie said, sneering at Peter.

"Though, I'm kind of mad that you tricked me into getting here. Why did you do that?"

"Yeah, why?" Peter asked.

"I don't know what to say," Santori began, "other than when I found out there was a whole other world out there, I was desperate to get out of Zentobia and see it. I've lived for too long with my father and brother, who only care about themselves and power. I didn't want to miss the chance to break free and see what real life could be like."

Peter rolled his eyes.

Maggie threw her arms around their new visitor.

"We're going to have to put this chat on hold and get home," their dad said sternly. "Your mother is anxiously waiting to see us, and I need to get to the police station. Let's go."

They walked in silence until Peter grabbed Santori's arm. "You just met your mother. How could you leave her?"

Santori lowered her head. "It wasn't a simple decision. I know I will see her again. You don't understand what it's like back there with my father."

"Well, he kidnapped my sister, so I have an idea."

Santori reached to grab Maggie's hand, who grasped it tightly. She looked over at Peter with a huge smile and a gleam in her eye.

On the walk home, Maggie daydreamed about bringing Santori to school with her. Her dad's mumbling interrupted her thoughts. He muttered different ways to tell McCall they might have unwelcome visitors from another world coming to invade their town. Peter trailed behind, giving Santori dirty looks. *What's his problem?*

A loud humming from above broke the uncomfortable silence.

"Wow! What's that in the sky?" Santori pointed overhead.

"It's an airplane," Maggie said. "People are in it. They're all flying to another city."

"People don't fly on their own here? They have to be inside something? That's weird."

"Yep, people can't fly here, and animals can't talk." Maggie nudged Santori's elbow and smiled.

As their house came into sight, Maggie ran toward the driveway. "Come on, guys. Let's go!" She couldn't wait to see her mother and Bacon. She jumped up the steps that led to the front door and tried to turn the knob. She knocked and then pounded her fists into the door. Bacon's barks were so loud she had to cover her ears.

"Mom!" she screamed. "We're home." She turned to her father, who walked up behind her. "Dad, the door is locked. Where's Mom?"

Her dad took the key out of his pocket. "I don't know." He opened the door, and they all stepped inside.

Bacon jumped on Maggie and Peter, licking their hands. Maggie picked Bacon up and gave him a big kiss. Their dad searched the house for their mom.

"I know it's not the palace," Maggie said to Santori. "Hopefully, you'll get used to it."

Santori looked around. "I love it. I've never been anywhere outside of the palace, so this is amazing. I can't wait to see the rest of it."

"Maggie, why don't you give our visitor a tour and get something to eat," her dad said when he walked back into the room. "I need to find your mother. Peter, go get something to eat too."

Peter shook his head and headed upstairs to his room.

"Are you hungry?" Maggie asked Santori. "I can make us peanut-butter-and-jelly sandwiches."

"Sure. I have never had that before."

"Are you serious? They're so good. Come on, I'll show you how to make them." Maggie took her hand, and they went to the kitchen.

Griffen sat on the couch and called Penny's cell phone. She answered on the first ring.

"Griffen! Where are you? Are you okay? Are the kids okay?" Her screams echoed through the phone.

"Yes. We're all okay. We're at the house. Where are you?"

"I'm at the police station. I was going crazy waiting at home, so I came to talk to McCall. What happened?"

"It's a long story. I'll tell you everything, but I'm going to come down there and tell you and McCall at the same time. Stay put. I'm on my way."

"What about the kids? Can you bring them?" she asked.

"That's not a good idea," he began, "because they brought...um...a visitor back with them."

"What do you mean, they brought a *visitor* back?"

"I'll explain everything when I get there. Let McCall know I'm on my way. See you soon." He hung up and went to find Peter.

Peter stared out the window, replaying in his mind the adventure in Zentobia. His dad walked in and interrupted the memory.

"You okay?" His dad sat on the bed. "You look like you have something on your mind."

"Besides the fact that we just escaped from a madman in another world and his daughter is sitting in our kitchen? Oh, and you should know that if Cyrus and Krado make it here, they won't be able to find the rainbow to go back to Zentobia."

"What do you mean? I think Cyrus will figure out that if he can get here when it rains, he'll have someone on Zentobia make it rain so he can go back and forth. Or, he will somehow convince Minka to tell him."

"No, it's not that. When we first got to Zentobia, Minka told us that Mr. Walric couldn't find the rainbow's end to get home because he didn't drink a special potion before he left. Anyone that doesn't drink the elixir can't find their way back to the rainbow—ever."

His dad stood and paced the room. "That means that Cyrus will need us to get him back to the rainbow's end. We can use this to our advantage. I know this experience has been very traumatic, but I will figure out what to do next. We'll get Santori back to Zentobia, and things will go back to normal around here."

"That's good, because I don't trust her." Peter stood and walked over to his desk. "I think she's up to something."

"What makes you say that?"

He couldn't get the vision of Santori holding hands with Maggie and smirking at him out of his head. "I don't have any proof yet. But I'll get it."

"Okay, but be careful, because we still have a lot to learn about Zentobia and Santori. She is the daughter of *Cyrus*.

I'm going to head to the police station now to see your mother and the sheriff. We'll figure this out." He patted Peter's back and headed toward the door. "Don't leave the house, and keep an eye on the girls while I'm gone."

"Don't worry, Dad. I'll watch them like a hawk."

"Good."

Peter followed behind his dad and peered down the stairs. He sat, listening to Maggie and Santori chat in the kitchen below.

CHAPTER THIRTY-FIVE

Griffen walked into the police station and headed straight for McCall's office.

Penny ran over. "I'm so happy to see you. I can't wait to lay my eyes on the kids. Are you sure they're okay? I want to hear everything that happened."

He wrapped his arms around her. "They're okay, but we have to plan our next move." He grabbed her hand and walked into McCall's office. She took a seat in one of the empty chairs in front of the desk.

"I hear you discovered another world. I can't wait to find out everything about it." McCall plopped into his over-sized chair. "I had a little time for this to sink in. This is tremendous news. It's a big deal for our little town. Once people find out about it, they'll all want to see the rainbow's end and cross through that portal. That is, if it doesn't keep disappearing on us."

Griffen sat next to Penny. He glared at McCall with the same stern look he gave to Maggie and Peter when they came home with a bad grade. "We can't let anyone find out about it. Not only because we have a lot of investigating to do first, but no one can know about Zentobia. There's a lot at stake."

"That name sure sounds otherworldly. Look, news like this could put Hailsville on the map. We'll become a leading tourist destination and attract people from all over the country—heck, the world. Do you know what this could mean for our economy? And, in case you didn't notice, this town can use a few cosmetic updates."

Griffen knew it would take a lot of convincing to persuade McCall to keep a lid on this discovery. "We've got lives at stake here. More happened than me just going to get the kids and bringing them back here. There were other *people* there."

McCall stood from behind his desk. "This is even bigger than I thought. Are they green and alien-like?"

"No, they are not *green*. They look just like us. Their world is in chaos, and opposing rulers are at odds. One ruler —Minka—her daughter came back here with us, and it wasn't by our choice. Now, her father, Cyrus, is planning to come after her. He is evil and unpredictable, and we need to be ready for him."

McCall's jaw dropped. He walked over to the office door and closed it. He grinned and clasped his fingers together. "This just keeps getting better. I'm sure we can handle this Cyrus guy. What kind of evil are we talking about?"

Griffen filled in McCall on Cyrus's plans to use dark magic.

"Not sure we can go up against magic. We might need to bring in some back-up," McCall said.

That would be too many eyes on this case. "No, not yet. Let's see how this plays out first," Griffen said. "I think we've got it under control."

"This man sounds awful," Penny said. "I can't believe he had Maggie. He must have terrified her!"

"She's stronger than you think." Griffen stood. "But we need to stop him when he gets here. We should have at least two police officers stationed at the rainbow's end around the clock."

McCall walked back over to his desk and sat down. "Okay. When we get this Cyrus guy, I want to question him and find out more about his world. How are we going to get him to go back there if he is the one that controls the rainbow portal?"

Griffen explained that Cyrus would need him to get back to Zentobia since he didn't drink the memory potion. "Plus, we have his daughter. She needs to go back there with him."

"I'd like to find out more about these potions."

"Fine, but don't get sidetracked by any of that stuff. We need to focus on Cyrus."

"Okay, but I want to circle back around to this magic business. I'll get the two other members of the task force stationed at the rainbow's end right away. If anyone comes through that portal, we'll catch 'em."

"Speaking of other people going through the portal," Griffen began, "I found our missing people in Zentobia and brought them back here. They're going to come by the station tomorrow. They can fill you in on what happened."

"That's great news. What about these rainbow people we've been observing? Did they come from Zentobia? What were they doing here?"

Griffen recalled the promise he'd made to Minka to allow her people to continue to collect the soil. He had to lie to McCall.

"I think they were exploring our town and trying to fit in by looking like they were working."

"I guess that would explain all the digging we saw," McCall said. "Though, it was strange. Almost as strange as our town being connected to another world. We're going to have to figure that one out sooner than later...before anyone else stumbles through it."

Penny let out an anxious sigh and turned to Griffen. "Can we go home now and see the kids?"

"Yes, let's go." He welcomed the interruption. They headed to the door, and he turned to McCall. "Keep me posted. I'll be waiting."

CHAPTER THIRTY-SIX

Renault woke up disoriented, lying on the ground in Hailsville. The unusual vision of dark gray clouds floating in the sky caught his attention. When he sat up to take a closer look, water dripped down his face, and his clothes stuck to his body. He put his hands in the air to catch the rain. *It's clear. I made it. I'm in another world.* He stood and wobbled as he walked along a rocky trail. His shoes sank into puddles of water, making small splashes along the way. *I have no idea where to go to find Santori and Griffen, but exploring another world won't be too bad.*

After Maggie and Santori ate two peanut-butter-and-jelly sandwiches each, Maggie gave a tour of her house and saved her room for last.

"I'm sure my room is smaller than the one you have, but I like it." Maggie walked in. All her favorite things from her old house were there. Pictures of unicorns hung on the walls, and stacks of old toys that she didn't want to give away filled the corners.

"It's amazing." Santori went straight over to Maggie's desk and picked up a book. "You're like me. You like to read." She flipped through the pages, reading passages along the way.

"Yep, and I like to write." Maggie pulled out her journal and sat on the floor. "While you read that, I am going to write something in my journal really quick."

Things are getting better here. I closed the case on Mr. Drop, and I have a new friend named Santori. I think my detective skills are really improving. I found a carving of a book in a tunnel, and I saved a whole bunch of people from Santori's evil father. Maybe my dad will let me work with him on some cases. That would be really fun. I might not be writing as much now. Hmmm...maybe Peter was right to focus more on what's in front of me rather than just writing it all down.

She put her pen inside the journal and tucked it under her bed. "Can I ask you something?"

"Sure. What?"

"Umm...Your Dad freaked me out pretty bad. Did you get scared living with him?"

Santori paused before answering. "I'm sorry he did that to you. I don't think he would have hurt you. He didn't have a bad temper with me or Krado. I didn't want to know what he was like outside of our house, but I heard things from the other kids that were hard to ignore. I tried my best not to listen."

"Is that why you went to the south with your mom?"

"Yes, and because my father lied to me. Not to mention I wanted to get to know my mom. Can I tell you a secret? You can't tell anyone. Not even Peter."

Maggie tried to hide the excitement bursting within. "I won't tell. I promise. What is it?"

"Okay. Before I left, I found out my mom knows magic."

"Whoa...are you serious? Like real magic with spells and potions? Is that how the stairs in her palace are floating? Wait...do *you* know magic?"

Santori shrugged. "No. I wish I did. The stairs float because of my grandfather. He cast a spell on them a long time ago."

"That's *so* cool."

"She told me she doesn't use it anymore because it can be dangerous. No one practices it anymore."

Magic fascinated Maggie, and she had a collection of books to prove it. She had plenty of mystery books, but mostly ones that had girls with magical powers as their main characters.

Maggie sat up straight. "Can I tell *you* a secret?"

"I love secrets." Santori sat next to Maggie on the floor.

"When we went back to the south side of the world through the tunnels, I found something etched into the wall that looked like the outline of a book."

Santori's eyes widened. "Really?"

"Yes. But what was even more interesting is that it had the letter S on it and a big star." Maggie cocked her head. "Do you think the S could have stood for Santori?"

Santori laughed. "What would a carving of a book with my initial on it be doing in a wall in a tunnel?"

"I don't know, but if we ever go back there, we have to check it out." Maggie walked to her desk and picked up a book. "You know, if you come to school with me, you can go to the library and pick out your own books."

"What would we tell people at school if they ask where I'm from?"

"I doubt anyone will ask." Maggie averted her eyes. "I haven't made any good friends yet. But if they do, that's easy. We'll say you're my cousin visiting from home. My teacher knows I'm not from here."

"That sounds good. And, don't worry, I can help you make friends. I've had a lot of experience at that." Santori stood and looked down at her clothing, and then at Maggie's outfit. "I definitely don't have the right clothes."

Maggie walked over to inspect her attire. *Her outfit stands out. That's for sure.* The bright yellow-and-orange-striped top paired with a khaki green skirt that had black polka dots demonstrated a mismatched mess. The black leggings and chunky black boots were the only normal-looking things on her. If they were going to pull this off, Santori would have to outfit herself in the drab dress code the kids wore in school.

"My clothes are too small for you. I have an idea. But it's kind of sneaky. It might be the only way to get you something to wear." *Having a friend here will be worth it.*

"You should know *sneaky* is my middle name." Santori winked.

"Good, because I would normally never do something like this. We'll have to go to the mall. I think I know where my mom keeps some extra money. We can get you a plain top to wear with the leggings under your skirt. You'll fit in with something like that."

"That sounds amazing. How will we get there? Can we go now?" Santori walked toward the door.

Maggie followed. "Yeah, but we have to make sure Peter doesn't see. And we have to be fast before my parents get home. Be super quiet and follow me." She peered out her door to make sure the coast was clear. They tiptoed downstairs and into the kitchen.

Maggie went from cupboard to cupboard looking for the secret jar that stored money for a rainy day. *Where is it?* The last cabinet she opened held a solid yellow container. *Finally!* She took it down and pressed it against her side. When she twisted off the lid, a stack of bills fell onto the floor. *Yikes!* She bent to pick them up and stuffed two twenty-dollar bills into her pocket. *That should be enough. I'll pay Mom back.* After closing the lid, she put the jar back into the cupboard.

She turned to Santori and whispered, "The mall—which is actually just a shopping center with a few stores—is close to the house. We can walk there. Let's go."

A high-pitched squeak echoed in the room when Maggie opened the front door. Holding her breath, she closed it gently behind them. As they walked down the street, Santori trailed behind, sticking out her tongue to catch the rain in her mouth. Maggie turned back and played along, until she spotted her brother's frame staring at them from the living room window. *Oh no. Now we really have to get home before Mom and Dad.*

CHAPTER THIRTY-SEVEN

Larz, Leo, and Cafferdy, looking tired and haggard from the long journey back to the south side of Zentobia, burst into Minka's office and slumped onto a couch next to Talia and Chester.

Tears welled in Minka's eyes as she listened to Larz replay the events and describe the conditions of the prisoners. She could tell he muscled every bit of energy to fill her in on what had happened since he parted ways with Griffen in the tunnels.

"Cyrus is an awful man, but to keep all those people as his slaves is beyond cruel." She reached for a tissue to dry her eyes. "It's a good thing we rescued everyone."

"What do you mean? How did you know they were there?"

"Maggie saw them when Cyrus held her captive. She told us where they were being kept, and she went over there with Brit and Griffen to set them free. I think they were helping Cyrus program the weather machine to turn the last gold star black."

"I'm glad they're safe. But he'll just get more people."

"We're going to have to stop him once and for all." She stood and walked to her desk. "Something else happened while you were gone. Griffen and the kids went back to Hailsville, and Santori went with them. I sent Renault after her."

"This complicates things even more."

"It does, but I have a plan. I have something Cyrus wants." She looked up at the painting of her palace hanging on the wall. "I will make him think I will trade this side of the world for a life with my daughter and son."

"You're going to pretend to give up everything to have your kids back?"

Talia chirped frantically. Chester sprang up and trotted over to Minka's chair. He placed his front legs into her lap.

"Exactly. Besides, I learned a valuable lesson recently from a man from another world. Family means everything. I'm not willing to give that up a second time."

Larz opened his mouth to speak, but Minka cut him off. "I want you to round up the squirrels and locate the book of magic my father hid in the tunnels for me and find a spell that will take care of Cyrus. I will not let our people suffer from the likes of that beast."

"I don't think we'll need the squirrels, unless the location of the book moves."

"What do you mean?"

"On our way back, Maggie uncovered a carving etched into the wall that revealed an image of the book of magic."

Minka's eyes widened. "She saw a carving of the book?"

"She had no idea what it was. I had to take a second look because it was different from how I remembered it."

"That's not possible."

"The cover had the letter S etched into it."

She walked to Larz. "*Santori?* Why would my father do

that? If her initial is on the book, she might be the only one who can use it."

"I don't know. Maybe we won't even need it. Are you sure you want to open that door?"

"I already did when we got trapped in the tunnels. I'm just afraid if our people get a taste of magic again, the desire for a more dangerous kind will grow too strong, and it will tear us all apart. I don't want that to happen again and repeat history. That's why my father warned me that the danger of magic outweighs the reward. But now we have no choice." Minka headed toward the door. "My dad knew one day Cyrus would try to avenge his father's death. So he left me that book. At least, I thought he left it for me. Santori is not ready."

Just a few miles north of Minka's palace, Cyrus and Krado, along with their guards, were in the sky, fast approaching the border to the south.

"Look, up ahead. The border is clear," Krado said. "I wonder what dear ol' Mom is doing to get ready for us?"

"There is nothing she *can* do," Cyrus snickered, his cape flapping feverishly in the air. "She's no match for us."

"What are you going to do to her?" Krado raised his brows. "You're not going to kill her, are you? She *is* my mother."

Cyrus stopped in mid-air. "I'm not a monster. Why do people keep thinking I'm a monster?" *That was my father's way of doing things, not mine.* His feet wobbled at the thought of some of the evil actions his father took. *He would be proud of how much I have accomplished in this world. Wouldn't he?* "But there will be consequences for her behavior. She will pay a price, regardless of the fact that she's your mother."

Krado shrugged. "What if it wasn't *her* idea?"

Cyrus crossed his arms and faced Krado as they hovered. "Do you think one of her guards convinced Santori to go back with her? I'll kill him."

"No. That's not it. I think she wanted to go back with Mom to the south side of the world. She had a videograph of her under her pillow."

He threw his cape over his shoulders. Rage filled his veins, and his body trembled. "Where did she get that? And why are you just telling me about this?"

Krado backed up and ran his hand over his shoulder where the backpack strap rested. "I just found out and am telling you now." He removed the bag. "I've got to put this thing down somewhere. It's too heavy. Can we get to the palace?"

Cyrus turned south and flew ahead of Krado, anguishing over why Santori would choose to be with her mother. He gave her everything, he thought, and promised her a place alongside him and Krado when she turned sixteen. *What more could she want?* Preoccupied thinking about Santori, he didn't notice the palace below.

"There it is." Krado shook his head as if waking from a dream. "Wow, it's all real."

Cyrus, more alert now, flew up to Krado and snapped his fingers in front of his face. "Get ready. We have work to do." He signaled for everyone to land. "Let's go."

None of Minka's guards armed the gate, making their landing a breeze. They all moved swiftly up the walkway to the entrance of the palace.

CHAPTER THIRTY-EIGHT

The sound of laughter coming from the TV filled the living room in the Millers' home. Griffen and Penny opened the front door, and Peter didn't move a muscle. He had fallen asleep on the couch.

Penny ran straight to him, shook his arm, and whispered in his ear. "Wake up. I missed you."

Peter, dazed, opened his eyes. His mother knelt over him, brushing his hair back. He sat up and gave her a big hug. "Mom. I missed you too!"

"Where's your sister?" Penny looked around. She sat on the couch next to him. "I heard we have a visitor. I would like to meet her."

"They're not here."

Griffen walked over and sat down on the other side of him. "Where the heck are they? I thought you were monitoring them?"

"I did. That's how I know exactly where they are." Peter stood, crossed his arms, and faced his parents, eager to tell them what happened. "Maggie took money out of the secret hiding place, and they went shopping to buy Santori a shirt for school. She is planning to go to school with Maggie."

Griffen stood and crossed his arms. "Why did you let them leave the house?"

The bulging veins on his dad's forehead signaled he could explode at any moment. Peter had to choose his answer carefully, but he hadn't planned this far ahead. He simply wanted to prove Santori might not be as nice as she seemed. "Because I don't trust Santori. I think she's up to something. But Maggie actually came up with the idea. She wants her to go to school with her, and she said she needs the right clothes to fit in."

"The kids at school can be very cruel, but no one should have to change who they are to be accepted," Penny said.

"Has everyone lost their minds?" Griffen asked, pacing the room. "Santori can't stay here with us or go to school with Maggie. She has to go back."

Peter's stomach growled so loudly he bent his head to listen. "Good luck with that. I'm pretty sure she wants to see more of Hailsville first."

Penny walked over to Griffen and put her hand on his arm. "Is it such an awful idea to have Santori stay for a bit? It would be nice for Maggie to have a friend here."

Griffen threw his hands in the air and shook his head. "It would be great for Maggie to have a friend, but not the daughter of a malicious monster who kidnapped her. You weren't there. You didn't see this guy and what he did to Minka. He stole her children and told them she was dead. Minka can finally be with her daughter."

The front door opened, and Maggie and Santori walked in, shopping bags weighing down their hands.

"Speak of the devil," Griffen said, his eyes locked in their direction. "I thought I told you to stay put. What were you thinking, leaving the house? What if someone saw Santori and asked about her?"

Maggie smiled and looked at Santori. "That's easy. We have a plan. This is my cousin, visiting from home."

"That *is* a good idea," Penny said, rushing over to Maggie. She wrapped her arms around her, squeezing so tightly that Maggie let out a yelp. "Are you okay? Let me look at you." Penny let go and ran her eyes over Maggie from top to bottom. She turned her attention to Santori. "I'm Maggie's mother, Penny. We would love to have you stay with us, but I'm afraid it's not safe."

Maggie offered her best puppy-dog face that she used all too often. "But, Dad, pleeeaaasseee. What if she stays for only a day or two so she can go to school with me and see what it's like?"

Peter knew he would give in. *He always does.*

"Okay, she can stay. But just for a little while." Griffen put clenched fists on his hips. "And there will be rules to follow. No leaving the house without telling us first."

Maggie and Santori jumped up and down.

Peter walked over to his father. "Are you crazy?"

His dad shook his head. "Everything that's happened over the last couple days has been crazy."

Santori strutted alongside Peter, smiling. "Did you hear that, Peter? I get to stay." She nudged his arm. "Want me to make you a peanut-butter-and-jelly sandwich? I'm pretty good at them."

"No thanks. I can make my own." He rolled his eyes and went to the kitchen.

CHAPTER THIRTY-NINE

Minka sat on the couch in her office with Chester curled in her lap. The chubby dog had just eaten another meal. Little pieces of food hung from his nose, and drool dripped out of the sides of his mouth. Minka patted the drool with a tissue. She put the paper on the table, lifted a brush, and stroked his fur.

"How can you be so calm?" Larz asked. "Are you sure you're doing the right thing? There has to be another way. At least have more guards in here in case he tries something."

Minka shook her head. "This is the way it has to be." She flinched at the rattle of the palace doors. "They're here."

Cyrus, Krado, and an army of guards marched through the palace entrance, heading to war. They stopped in the foyer, and Cyrus looked around.

"This place is empty," Krado said. He held his hand up

to his mouth in the shape of a horn. "Hello? Is anyone here?"

Cyrus grabbed his arms and pushed them down. "What are you doing? Be quiet. Follow me. I know where to find her." *Minka is always predictable.*

They hustled down the hall toward Minka's office. As they approached, the sound of Chester snoring echoed off the walls.

Krado covered his ears with his hands. "What is that awful sound?"

They stepped inside. Cyrus turned back to his guards and held his hand out, signaling them to wait in the hall.

"This is how you plan to kill us? With a snoring dog?" Krado said to Minka.

"It's nice to see you, Krado," Minka said. "This is Chester. He snores after he eats."

"Geez, how much did he eat?" Krado chuckled.

"Enough small talk." Cyrus inched closer to the couch. "Where is Santori?"

Minka lifted Chester off of her lap and placed him on the floor. He snorted and turned onto his side. She stood and moved closer to Cyrus and Krado. Larz followed.

"You're wearing the gold cape. You must mean business. Santori is not here. She went to Hailsville with Maggie."

"What are you talking about? Bring her to me now!"

"Don't you remember the young girl you kidnapped? That was Maggie. Santori decided she didn't want to stay in Zentobia anymore. She wanted a normal life away from you."

Cyrus pulled the knife out of his belt and twirled it around. "I don't believe you. She would not leave me or Zentobia."

"Yeah, she would," Krado said to Cyrus. He turned to

Minka. "How'd they get there?"

"Enough!" Cyrus shouted. He stepped outside and addressed his guards. "Search the palace, and don't come back until you find Santori."

"They got there through a rainbow portal that you created, Cyrus." She approached him. "When you make it rain, it not only kills our land, but it opens a portal through the rainbow to another world. That's how Maggie and Peter got here. That's how Griffen got here, and that's how they all went back to Hailsville."

Cyrus recalled the story Maggie had told him about how she arrived in Zentobia through the rainbow. His heart raced faster than his flying shoes at full speed.

"This could change everything! I will go to this other world and get Santori back and maybe a few others." He brought the knife up to his eyes and looked at it like a fox circling its prey.

"I have a better option for you," Minka said. "I will go to Hailsville and remain there with Santori. Krado, you can come with me and see what it's like to live in another world. I will give you the south side of the world to rule. You'll have what you always wanted."

Cyrus stepped closer to Minka. "Why would you give up your side of the world to go to a place that you've never even been before? What's the catch?"

"There is no catch." She stepped back. "I'll have my kids, and you'll have Zentobia. Larz will be here to make sure you treat my people fairly. He'll be your second in command. And, if anything happens to him, you'll never see your kids again."

She turned to Larz, "You'll keep things in check for me here, okay?"

Larz nodded.

"I haven't agreed to any of this yet!" Cyrus roared. The rustling noise coming from Krado digging through his backpack distracted him. He turned to Krado. "What are you looking for?"

"I don't have enough stuff to travel. I knew I should have brought those other bags." Cyrus pulled the bag away from Krado and slammed it to the ground.

One of Cyrus' guards walked into the room and whispered that they couldn't find Santori. Cyrus crossed his hands and walked out into the hallway.

This is what my father always wanted. And now I can have it...Should I give up my children for it? I'll get them back. I will be the ruler of all Zentobia! When the time is right, I can go after this other world!

He slithered back into the room. "Krado, you're going to Hailsville with your mother."

Krado threw his hands up. "Whoa...You're just going to hand me over to her? Just like that? What about our plans and my rise to power alongside you?"

"It will still happen, but I'm delaying it. After I get the world up and running under my rule, I'll send for you."

"Fine. I'll be waiting." He turned to Minka. "Don't expect any mother-son bonding time. I'll be exploring a new world."

Minka smiled and walked over to her desk. She opened the top drawer and pulled out a gold key. She held it high and walked over to Cyrus. "This is the key to the palace. It will be yours once it rains so we can go through the portal."

Hypnotized by the dangling key, Cyrus shook his head and steadied his wobbling feet. "I'll head back to the north now and make some arrangements. Be ready to leave in the morning." He looked at Krado. "Let's go."

Cyrus, Krado, and their guards left the office and

headed back through the palace to the main entrance.

###

Minka grabbed the backpack from the chair behind her desk. She opened it, pulled out a small bottle of memory potion, and drank its contents.

"Are you going to give any of that potion to Krado?" Larz asked.

"No. It's too risky. The less he knows, the better. Just get the book of magic and figure out what spell to use to stop Cyrus. Once it's done, use the weather machine to make it rain so you can send Brit to Hailsville to find me and the kids. We'll all come back to Zentobia as one happy family."

"I hope this works."

"It has to."

###

Cyrus and Krado stood outside Minka's palace.

"Learn everything you can about this other world so we can use the information to our advantage when you get back here," Cyrus said. "Look at it as your first big assignment as my apprentice."

Krado perked up. "I can do that. What are you going to do here?"

"First, the south will get a big dose of rain tonight. Then, in the morning, I will introduce myself to the people on this side of the world and let them know I can stop the rain. They will be indebted to me and get a lesson on how things will work." Cyrus' boney body grew stronger as he spoke. He pulled the knife out of his belt and twirled it around. "Anyone who doesn't listen will pay the price."

CHAPTER FORTY

G riffen sat at the kitchen table, watching his phone. *Why haven't I heard anything? What is taking Cyrus so long to get here?*

Penny lifted a wooden spoon out of the pot on the burner, blew on it, and let the spicy pasta sauce fall onto her tongue. "Delicious. The kids will love it." She turned to Griffen. "Staring at the phone won't make it ring." She walked over to the cupboard and took out plates. "Help me set the table. We'll enjoy a family dinner."

He put his phone down and took the plates while Penny placed the silverware around the table. The clunking of the forks against the plates clashed with the sound of Griffen's phone ringing.

Griffen answered it on the first ring and walked into the living room. "McCall, you got anything?"

"Yeah, I need you down at the station. I want to go over this Zentobia business. People are asking questions."

"Okay, I'm on my way." Griffen went back into the kitchen to say goodbye to Penny. "Sorry, I'm going to have to miss dinner. McCall wants to meet. Save some pasta for me, okay?"

"I will. Be careful." She ran over to give him a quick hug goodbye.

Santori heard Penny call "dinner's ready," and she ran downstairs with Maggie.

"It smells so good," Santori said. "I'm starving. Where should I sit?"

"You can sit here." Penny pointed to a chair. "Where's Peter?"

"In his room," Maggie began, "being antisocial. I'll go get him." She ran up the stairs.

Santori sat, her eyes stuck on Penny as she served the pasta. "It must be nice for Maggie to have you to cook for her. She's very lucky."

Penny sat next to Santori and smiled. "Thank you. You're very lucky to have found your mother."

Maggie and Peter's loud banter interrupted the conversation.

"I don't care what you think, Peter, we still have open cases that need to be solved. We need to find out more about Zentobia. And we have the mystery of the rainbow's end and why it's in Hailsville. I'm going to help figure these out," Maggie said.

"Maybe you should leave that up to the professionals, like Dad," Peter said. "But if he wants our help, I might be willing to offer my experience."

"Sit down," their mom said. "Let's enjoy dinner."

"Where's Dad?" Maggie asked.

"He's at the police station checking in with the sheriff."

Penny stared down at her plate. "Try the pasta. I made it with homemade sauce."

Maggie shoved such an enormous spoonful of pasta into her mouth that sauce dripped down the side of her face.

After dinner, Peter trailed behind Maggie and Santori up to Maggie's room. He stood in the doorway, his arms crossed in front of his chest.

Maggie yanked a bed out of the couch and sat on it. She pulled Santori next to her. "You can sleep here." She turned to Peter. "You look like you have something to say."

"Yeah, it's been bothering me since we got back." He walked over to Santori. "I get what you said about why you wanted to come to Hailsville. But your dad kept prisoners in his palace and is trying to bring back dark magic and control everyone. Don't you want to stop him? Or do you just not want to be around when it happens? Your mom will still be there, you know."

The color drained from Santori's face. "I didn't know he was doing any of that. If I did, I would have tried to talk to him and get him to change his mind. I need some time to think about this. I might have made a mistake coming here." She faced Maggie. "Actually, there is no time. I have to go back to Zentobia. My mom could be in danger. I think everyone in my world is in danger."

Maggie grabbed Santori's hand. "But you just got here."

"I know, but this is such a mess...."

"A huge mess," Peter said. *Which is why it's the perfect time for you to go home.*

"I need to go back."

Maggie stood. "Then we'll go with you to help."

187

"We'll what?" Peter stepped in front of Maggie. *I should have known Maggie would want to go too!*

"You heard me. We're going back to Zentobia to help Santori save her world. She needs us."

"What about Mom and Dad? They would kill us if they found out." *I really don't want to go back there. Besides, I told Minka I was not coming back for a really long time.*

"Good thing Dad's at work. Plus, it's nighttime. We'll stuff the beds with pillows and sneak out. We can be home by morning." Maggie grabbed her bag off the floor and filled it with essentials. "This time, I'm planning ahead."

"That's an ambitious timeline," Peter said. *There is no way we can do this in one night. Can we?*

Santori approached Maggie. "Are you sure you want to go? I don't know what will happen once we get there."

"First, we need to find that factory where Cyrus keeps that crazy machine," Peter said.

"Wait...you are going too?" Maggie asked.

"Um, yeah...I can't let you go there alone. Besides, I can get him back for kidnapping you."

"Wow, Peter, I didn't think you had it in you," Santori said.

Peter's lips formed a quirky half smile. "Funny. I'll go pack a bag. Mom and Dad should be asleep by eleven p.m. Let's head out then."

Maggie's mind raced with different scenarios of what to do when they arrived in Zentobia. Her alarm buzzed at eleven p.m., and she nudged Santori, who lay wide awake on the extra bed. "Let's go."

She put her backpack over her shoulders, and they met Peter in the hallway.

As they tiptoed down the stairs, creaks echoed in the air.

"I hope these old stairs don't wake Mom and Dad up," Maggie whispered.

"They'll get up if you keep talking," Peter said.

The front door stood just a few inches away, and Maggie darted for the doorknob. She crept outside, and the others treaded softly behind.

"Phew! We made it out of the house," Maggie said. "Step one is done."

"How many steps are there?" Peter asked.

Maggie pulled a sweater out of her bag. *Glad I brought this. It wasn't this cold last time.* "I don't know, but a lot."

No one said a word the rest of the way to the rainbow's end.

When they got close, Peter broke the silence. "We need a plan when we get to Zentobia." He turned to Santori. "Do you know where the factory is located? Do you think we can sneak inside and find that machine? All we need to do is figure out how to make it not work and then sneak out."

Santori paused. "I know where it is. When Krado and I were little, we used to play around there. It's not too far from the palace. We won't have flying shoes, so we'll have to go through the north on foot. Don't worry, I know some shortcuts."

The familiar rocks that led up to the rainbow's end caught Peter's eye. He ran past them and closer to the location where the lights came streaming out of the ground. "Oh no. It's not here. But I see something else."

Snoring bellowed from two police officers sleeping under a tree.

"What is it?" Maggie came up from behind. She covered her ears to drown out the sound. "Oh. Yikes! Just be quiet, and hopefully they won't wake up. Just because the rainbow isn't here this second doesn't mean it won't appear. Let's wait."

Santori sat on a nearby rock to rest her tired legs and drank from her water bottle.

Peter joined her. "I think it's pretty brave of you to do this."

"Is that actually a *compliment*? Thank you. I rarely stand up to my father, but now that I have a mother, I don't want to lose her." Light beams from the ground caught her gaze. "Look! There it is."

She shot up and grabbed Maggie's shoulder. "Ready?"

"Yep." Maggie reached for Santori and Peter's hands. "Let's all go together."

They marched into the lights, and within a matter of seconds, they were on their way to Zentobia.

CHAPTER FORTY-ONE

P eter opened his eyes to see the faces of Maggie and Santori staring down at him as he lay on the ground in Zentobia. *Here we go again.*

"Wake up, sleepy head. We're on a time schedule." Santori pulled Peter up by his arms. "Follow me. I'll get us to that factory without being seen."

The group trekked through the outskirts of little towns. Lights were dim or not on at all in the homes they passed. A few times Peter thought he saw groups of people off in the distance.

A cluster of tall buildings came into view, and Santori turned a corner. "This way. It's a shortcut." She ran down a long flight of stairs.

At the bottom, she skirted past a few doorways and stopped at the last visible door. She opened it and walked into a small, dark room. A scratched up black box rested against the wall. "It's still here." She lifted the top of the box, and a silver button appeared. She turned to Maggie and Peter. "I just have to press this button and our ride to the factory will appear."

Her fingertips pressed lightly on the button. Outside the room, a sleek walkway emerged from below the ground.

"Whoa...that looks like one of those people movers at the airport," Maggie said. "Except I don't see any tracks in front of it or behind it."

"Krado and I discovered it years ago when we ditched school and came down here to play. It's a glider. We found a few others too that go to different places." Santori left the room and climbed onto it. "It's been a while since I've ridden it. Hurry. Get on before it takes off."

Maggie jumped on and steadied her feet. "Good thing it has a railing to hold."

Peter grabbed the bar, and it took off. "This thing goes fast."

"It does. Just watch your head in case you have to duck under any walls," Santori said.

"Oh great. Thanks for the warning." Peter bent his knees to make himself smaller.

They sped through empty, underground corridors and bobbed up and down like they were riding a small roller coaster. Peter ducked every so often out of reflex to avoid any walls that might loom above.

After several minutes, the glider came to a halt, and Santori jumped out. "We're here. Follow me."

She led them through a short hallway and out a door. A dark building several feet away came into view.

"Is that the factory?" Maggie reached for her journal.

Peter shot her a disapproving look. "This is one of those times when your journal will slow us down."

"I see your point." She put it away.

"Yes. That's it," Santori said. "Keep an eye out for any guards."

"After you," Peter said. *And don't try any funny stuff.*

Santori led Maggie and Peter to the back of the building. The doorknob turned when she twisted it. "That's strange. No guards, and the door is unlocked."

They all entered.

"Which way?" Peter asked.

"We'll have to conduct a search." Maggie walked to the right. "Maybe we should split up. That's a common tactic for detectives."

"Nope. Not a good idea." Peter grabbed Maggie's arm. *Santori got us here, but I still don't trust her.*

"Okay, it just might take longer if we stay together."

"Let's start over here." Santori led Maggie and Peter in and out of several rooms. Many were empty, and all sorts of laboratory equipment occupied others.

"I don't even want to know what's in those test tubes." A rustling noise caught Peter's attention. "Hey, I hear something over there. Let's check it out."

They tiptoed down the hall and peered into a room at the end. A machine with steam coming out of the top sat in the center. Rows of oversized, illuminated buttons and heavy-looking levers ran up and down the sides of it.

"This has to be it!" Maggie bolted toward the machine. "Now how do we break it?"

Whispers from the hallway signaled someone's approach.

"Oh no! Do you guys hear that? Hide!" Maggie whispered.

They crouched behind a tall cabinet in the back of the room just in time before two people entered.

"I'm leaving in the morning for the south." Cyrus took off his cape and draped it over his arm. "Keep the rain going all night, and check in on the machine in the morning. Minka underestimated me. She might have freed my prisoners, but that's just a minor setback. With the final star black, I can bring back my father. He'll be so proud of all I've done. Together, we'll fulfill his dream of ruling Zentobia."

Peter's eyes grew as wide as a basketball.

Maggie placed a hand over her mouth to stop the shriek about to come out.

Santori's heels pushed into the floor so hard they looked like they might dig a hole.

Peter cringed when a noise from her boot scraping the floor rang through the room. *Yikes. I hope no one heard that.*

"What was that sound?" Cyrus asked the guard.

"I don't know. Maybe it came from the machine."

Peter peered from behind the cabinet. Cyrus and the guard were inspecting the machine. Peter ducked back down when he thought the guard looked his way.

"Strange. Everything here looks to be operating okay," the guard said. "Must have come from outside."

"Good. I don't want anything to interfere with tomorrow. Let's go." Cyrus and the guard left the room. Their voices faded into the background.

"That was close! I can't believe what I just heard." Peter ran over to the machine and examined a control panel on the front. "We don't have much time. Let's figure out how to break this thing and get out of here." A swishing noise came from above, causing him to look up. "What if we remove those balls spinning at the top? They look kind of important because they keep turning."

"We can try it." Maggie extended her arm, but it fell short. "I'm not tall enough to reach it. Wait...what if one of those causes the rain and the other is for the gold star? We need the rain to get home."

"Maggie's right. We can't break both of them. How do we know which one to choose?" Peter asked.

"I'll get up there and take a look." Santori brought a chair over from across the room and stood on it. "Well, this is interesting. One ball is orange and the other is black. The orange has to be for the rain. We should take the black one, because it's probably for the black star." Her hand barely touched the round ball. But after a few tries, her fingers yanked it free. She placed it inside her pocket. The swishing stopped, and steam no longer escaped from the top of it. A sharp clunk echoed through the room.

"I think you did it, or at least did something *bad*," Peter said.

"Yes! Mission accomplished. Now let's get out of here before someone hears that rattling noise." Maggie ran for the exit and the others followed.

At the door, Santori put a hand on Maggie's shoulder. "I can't go back with you."

"Why?" Maggie grabbed Santori's hand and held it. "You have to come back with us."

"No, she really doesn't," Peter said. *This plan is working like a charm. Don't ruin it.*

"I need to be with my mom and help her figure out what to do with my father," Santori said. "There's too much at stake for me to leave again now. Do you understand?"

"Yes, we get it," Peter said. "How are we going to get back to the rainbow?"

Maggie smacked his arm. "Seriously, Peter!" She turned to Santori. "I understand, but I will worry about you here. What if your dad finds out it was you and me and Peter that did this?"

"He won't. I'm going to sneak into my room, pack my bag, then head to my mom's palace. I think we might have stopped my dad. At least for a while." She hugged Maggie. "Thank you both for your help. But you need to go now. I'm going to give you flying shoes so you can get back while it's still raining."

Maggie's wide eyes looked at Peter. "OMG, Peter, you are going to love flying!"

"Um, yeah, that sounds cool." *Bonus! Another good thing came out of this trip.* "How are we going to get them without anyone seeing us?"

"Leave that up to me. I'll bring the shoes to where the glider dropped us off. Ride it to where we got on, then fly the rest of the way to the rainbow."

"Okay, see you there," Maggie said.

Maggie and Peter took off across the field to the building with the glider.

Santori sprinted in the opposite direction.

Maggie looked back at Peter. "I wonder where she's going to get the shoes?"

"Who cares as long as we get them and get out of here."

They slowed their pace as they approached the door to the building.

Peter grabbed the handle, and they ran inside. The air escaped his lungs. "I'm exhausted. This rainbow-hopping and saving the world takes a lot of work. Let's have a seat and just wait."

"Or we could investigate this building." Maggie took out her journal and inspected the area.

"Have at it." Peter plopped his tired body on the floor and slumped against the wall. "I'm not moving."

After what seemed like hours, Santori came bursting through the door. "I got them." She handed each of them a pair of flying shoes. "You'll have to show Peter how to use these, because I have to go before I get caught." She hugged Maggie again and then turned to Peter.

"Um...it's been great." Peter put up his hand in a high-five motion, but he could tell Santori didn't understand. "Okay, nevermind. Thanks for the shoes...we'll see you around."

"Yeah, I'll kinda miss you, Peter." She turned to Maggie. "And, of course, I'll miss you most of all." She walked to the room with the box to start the glider. It rose from below ground. "You guys are all set." She bolted out the door.

Maggie's eyes watered, and she lowered her head.

"No time for crying." Peter grabbed Maggie's hand and pulled her onto the people mover. "You can show me how to use these shoes on the way there."

Maggie spent several minutes going over everything she remembered about the shoes. In the middle of her explanation, the glider slowed down. "Um, Peter...what's happening? Why is this thing slowing down?"

They crept along inch by inch until the mover made a loud screeching stop, jolting them off their feet.

A clunking sound in the distance prompted Peter to put on the flying shoes. "Get your shoes on in case we need to fly the heck out of here."

The glider sprang forward, and Maggie's shoe fell to the opposite side, half of it hanging off the edge. "Oh no!" She darted to it, and her fingertips grasped it just in time. The glider took off at full speed, and she rolled to the edge, her legs dangling off the side. "Peter! Help!"

"I can't reach you! If I let go, I'll fly off this thing. Try to grab the arm of the railing and throw your legs up on the glider! Fast!"

Maggie's nails dug into the floor. She maneuvered her

hands toward the arm that connected the handrail to the bottom of the glider. "I can't get to it! It's too far away."

Peter extended his leg. "Grab my leg!"

Maggie pushed her arm as far forward as she could. Her hand clamped around Peter's shoe. "I got it!"

Peter used all his strength to pull back his leg.

Maggie heaved her body onto the glider and rolled over, gasping for air. "Can we get off this thing now?"

They sat in silence on the floor, clutching the handlebar the rest of the way.

⛪

Maggie and Peter jumped off the glider and raced up the stairs. Outside, darkness and orange rain surrounded them, and according to Maggie's watch, it would soon be morning in Hailsville.

"We don't have much time." Maggie put on her shoes. "Are you ready to try this? Just remember, the key is to focus."

"How hard can it be?" He tapped his left foot three times, and his body lifted from the ground.

Maggie giggled at the sight of Peter wobbling from side to side. His body flipped over into a somersault.

"Oh boy. You didn't tell me how difficult it is to balance," Peter said.

Maggie flew behind him and grabbed his hand. "Just until you get steady, then I'll let go." The rain came down faster, and she squinted to see straight ahead. "Everything is blurry. I can't tell which direction to go. Can you?"

Peter scoured the sky. "No. I don't see the rainbow anywhere! I'll fly ahead and look."

"No. We need to stay together."

Peter released his hand. "Sorry. We're running out of time. Just hover in the air or something and I'll be right back." He sped away, twisting and turning as he flew.

A few minutes passed, and Peter didn't return. The muscles in Maggie's stomach tightened. "Peter! Peter!" *UGH. When he gets back here, I am never talking to him again!* Her mind raced with thoughts of Cyrus swooping in and grabbing her.

Something bumped into her from behind and she sprang forward. "Ouch." She turned around, and Peter hovered next to her. "Don't leave me like that!"

"Sorry. It was our best option. I found the rainbow. Follow me."

They flew for several minutes until rays of light peered through the sheets of rain.

"I see it," Maggie said. "Race you!" Maggie took off in front. High-pitched noises coming from Peter trying to steady himself caused her to turn around. He gained momentum and passed her.

I'll show him. I have a secret trick I didn't tell him about. She tapped both feet together and sped up, waving back to him as she passed his side. "See you there."

Maggie slowed her pace as she approached the ground and turned to see Peter flying too fast behind her. *Oh no. I forgot to tell him how to land.* "Tap your right foot twice to slow down!" she yelled at him as she landed at the base of the rainbow.

"What did you say?"

"I said tap your right foot twice to land!"

Peter plummeted to the ground. "Ouch! You could have told me sooner how to land in these things."

She helped him up. "Sorry. It gets easier. Let's go while we still have the chance."

"Yeah. I want to get out of this world before something else bad happens."

They walked to the end of the rainbow and jumped inside with their flying shoes snug on their feet.

CHAPTER FORTY-TWO

Santori snuck into the palace to pack a bag. Already out of breath, she ran to her room, looking over her shoulder on the way. *I can't get caught.* She found a small suitcase tucked in her closet and filled it with a few essentials. Before she left, she thought about leaving a message for Krado but decided against it. *He'll figure it out soon enough.*

The flight to the south side of the world took her last bit of energy. Her heavy eyelids struggled to stay open until her mom's palace appeared below. She glided down to the front door.

Not a guard in sight.

She knocked on the door.

After a moment, the door opened, and Chester's droopy head peered through. "Miss Santori. You're back. I will fetch Minka."

"Is she asleep? I don't want to wake her."

The tired dog snorted. "She will want to see you. Please come inside. Follow me."

"Can I go to my room?"

"Yes. I think your mom is in there. Do you remember where it is?"

Santori nodded and made her way up the floating stairs to her room. She went in and found her mom sleeping in her bed.

Santori snuggled up next to her and rested her head on Minka's shoulder. "Mom?"

Minka rolled over and opened her eyes. "Santori! You came back. I've been so worried."

"I'm sorry. Everything just happened so fast, I didn't know what to do first."

"I understand. I don't think your father will, though. He'll be here in the morning. I planned to go to Hailsville with Krado to find you."

Santori stood. "I don't think you'll have to worry about Dad coming over or bothering us for a while."

Minka inched her body up alongside the headboard. "Why?"

"Well, I had a little help from Maggie and Peter. We snuck in the factory and found the machine he's using, and I took this from it." She pulled the ball out of her pocket.

Minka touched it. "Did anyone see you? Does Cyrus know you have this?"

"No. But we left an orange sphere on the machine. That one must control the rain."

Minka patted the bed, signaling for Santori to join her. "Cyrus must never know we have this."

"Okay, but there's something else. When we were there, I overheard Dad saying that he wants to bring his father back."

Minka cleared her throat and reached for the water on the dresser. "Now it makes sense why he was so determined to use dark magic. If Fydar comes back, the world will never be the same."

Santori rested her head on Minka's shoulder, slowly drifting off to sleep. Her grip on the round ball loosened.

Minka took it from Santori's hand and tucked it away in her pocket.

Krado put the last of his bags by the front door of Cyrus's palace and headed to the kitchen to fill up on more tigwats before his journey to Hailsville.

Faint voices from the end of the hallway grew louder as two guards came into view.

"What's going on?" Krado asked.

"There's a problem. We need to find Cyrus," one guard said. "Have you seen him?"

"No, but have you tried his office? That's usually where he is this time of morning. As his guards, shouldn't you know where he is at all times?"

The guards frowned. They headed straight for Cyrus's office.

Inside his office, Cyrus sat behind his desk, staring at a videograph of himself and his father. He stuffed it inside a drawer as soon as the guards entered.

"We have a situation," one guard said.

"What kind of problem could we have on this glorious day? I'm about to get the keys to the south side of the world."

The guards averted their eyes.

One stepped forward. "Someone has tampered with the machine. I'm afraid one of the sensors is missing."

Cyrus stood and slammed his fists into the desk. "What did you say?"

"A sensor of the mach..."

"I heard you!" With heavy fists, he smashed the papers from his desk onto the floor. "I was just there last night, and everything was fine. Where was the guard on duty? Which sensor is missing?"

"The black one," a guard said. "We've got everyone on this, Cyrus." The guard stepped back in line with the other one.

"This could ruin everything! I can't do anything without that sensor." Cyrus marched to the front of his desk and faced the guards. "You find out who did this and bring them to me. NOW!"

The guards bolted to the door and bumped into Krado, who was chewing on a tigwat as he entered.

"What's going on?" Krado asked.

Cyrus clenched his jaw so tightly his mouth ached. "We have a situation. Someone tampered with my machine. You won't be going to Hailsville today."

A piece of tigwat flew out of Krado's mouth. "What are you going to do?" He took a seat in front of Cyrus's desk.

"*We* have a lot to do to fix this mess. I think it's time you took on a larger role here. And you'll begin by figuring out who took that sensor."

Krado sat straight up and folded his hands in his lap. "I'm ready."

Cyrus took the tigwat from Krado's hand and threw it in the trash. "Good. Let's get started."

Maggie and Peter raced into their house just as the sun rose in the distance.

Peter closed the door behind him and exhaled. "I can't believe we pulled this off."

"Neither can I. I couldn't have done this without you." Maggie headed upstairs.

"What do you mean?"

"Did you forget you saved my life like three times? You saved me from Cyrus, on the glider, and you found the rainbow to get us home."

"Oh, yeah. All that. I guess I was pretty brave, huh? But we never could have done any of this without your keen detective skills."

"We make a great team. I just hope Cyrus doesn't find out Santori has a piece of his machine. Otherwise, we might have to go back there to save her."

"Oh, no. I am *not* going back there. That place is way too dangerous."

They burst out laughing.

Their mom stopped them before they reached the top of the stairs. "Maggie? Peter? What are you guys doing up so early?"

Maggie clenched her jaw. *Oh no, we're busted!* "Morning, Mom. Peter and I went out on an early morning walk. We missed Mr. Drop, so we thought the walk would remind us of him."

Their mom raised a brow and smiled. "That's sweet. Where's Santori?"

Maggie's stomach twisted in knots. She crossed her fingers behind her back. "She decided to leave in the middle of the night. I think she wanted to get to know her mom."

"I can understand that," their mom said. The sun peered through the window, and its reflection bounced off the silver flaps on Maggie and Peter's shoes and into her eyes. She looked down. "What are you wearing on your feet?"

I forgot we still have these flying shoes on!

"We made these shoes to remind us of Zentobia. We miss it there too. Gotta go get ready for school." She turned and raced to her room. Peter followed behind.

"Do you think she bought it?" Maggie asked.

"I don't know, but we better not wear these shoes to school. It's already going to be a long day without having to explain why we have wings on our shoes to everyone."

Maggie smirked. "True. Let's try them out after school and see if they work here. As long as no one sees us, what can go wrong?"

"Are you really asking that?" Peter sighed. "Who knows if these things have some kind of tracker in them. What if Santori got them from Cyrus's palace? The last thing we need is him figuring out two pairs of his flying shoes are in Hailsville."

"Don't be ridiculous. There's no way a tracker can find something in a different world, right?"

Peter raised his brows. "They have magic there. Who knows what else they can do?"

"Fine. Let's hide them for now, and we can see if they work later."

"Much later." Peter went to his room.

Maggie took off the shoes and tucked them under her bed. *Should be safe under there.*

She flipped through her journal and stopped at the description she'd written of the book etched into the tunnel wall. It troubled her. *The letter S. What if it does stand for Santori?* Her heartbeat quickened. *What if there's a real book somewhere in that tunnel that was meant for her to find? What if it's a book about magic?* She put the journal under her bed next to the flying shoes. *I think we have a new case to solve, and this one might be the biggest one yet. I better not tell Peter until after school. It's going to take a lot more than flying shoes to get him to go back to Zentobia.*

ABOUT THE AUTHOR

Routine trips to Disneyland with her daughter might have played a small role in Stacy D'Alessandro's passion for storytelling. Her daughter inspired the idea for *Journey to Zentobia* on a road trip home from one of their visits to the happiest place on Earth. They would pass a piece of paper back and forth in the car and each write part of a story. Her daughter's idea for a brother and sister to transport back in time through a rainbow portal stuck with Stacy for almost two years before she sat in front of the computer and began to write this book.

Though Stacy changed her daughter's original idea of the main characters going back in time to ending up in another world, the credit still goes to her daughter's innovative, young mind.

Learn more at stacydalessandro.com

Made in the USA
Las Vegas, NV
17 November 2021

34702107R00125